Ruby Milk

Lucy English

For Sam and Arlo

ACKNOWLEDGMENTS

Thank you to my sons, Sam and Arlo, for your patience and for inspiring me to be my best. Thank you to my editors, Adam Krause and Christine LePorte; this would have been nonsense without you. Thank you to friends Howard Lerner, Jean Ann Schulte, Laura Avakian, and Brant Hadfield for tolerating my lunacy and believing in me. Thanks to Deanne Smith for the wonderful cover design.

LEARN MORE

www.pennywademysteries.com

FOLLOW PENNY WADE

on Twitter @pennywadeboston
on Pinterest www.pinterest.com/
pennywadelsw

CHAPTER ONE

The gurney hit a raised section of sidewalk and a covered body bounced off. A collective gasp and one short, high-pitched cry rose from the small crowd gathered on the street. One of the emergency crew, a guy with an unkempt 2013 Red Sox Nation beard, caught the body and slid it back onto the gurney.

"Don't they strap 'em down?" I asked. I looked around and found I was talking to no one. The only people on the street were the group of bystanders waiting near an ambulance a few buildings from where I'd stopped.

Lights from the emergency vehicles flashed in the gray evening and bounced off brick and stone apartment buildings.

I only stood there a minute. The cold rose right through the soles of my ballet flats all the way up my spine. The last time I'd seen a body removed from a house I'd been on the inside looking out.

I turned and tramped in the other direction down the glazed street, shaking my head to clear the memory. At the end of the block, I could still hear intermittent static noises from the emergency crew's radios. I looked over my shoulder and saw the EMTs loading the body into the ambulance. I straightened my spine and turned once again to hurry home.

As I started to round the corner, I heard a wail—a woman's voice, both high and resonant—ricocheting off the buildings, chasing me down the block. I looked back up the street at the people gathered by the ambulance. The woman's cries continued in long waves broken by short silences. I couldn't see her, and I wanted to run back up the street toward her, but my legs wouldn't cooperate. It was as if my shoes had frozen to the icy sidewalk. Sweat pricked my armpits. I saw my ragged breath in the frigid air and decided I'd stood there long enough.

I sucked in some of the frosty air and jogged up the block. When I got close I slowed to a walk, edging around the group of people until I could see the woman. A large man stood next to her holding a blanket around her shoulders. I spotted a police officer and approached him.

"Officer, my name is Penny Wade," I said. He didn't look my way. "I'm a social worker at Community Counseling Services. Can I help?"

"No thank you, ma'am," he replied crisply, eyes still on the crew by the ambulance. "We have a staff social worker on location." He aimed his ample chin at the man with the blanket and walked away.

The woman's sobbing quieted. Her narrow face was drawn. The man wasn't talking to her, he was merely standing watching the EMTs. My heart twisted a little, but the situation was in the hands of the authorities. There was nothing for me to do.

I meandered over toward them anyway. The woman had become still, staring blankly in the direction of a man with graying blond hair and wire-rimmed glasses. The man took off his glasses, wiped them on his shirt, and replaced them. He ran his hand through his hair repeatedly and watched the EMTs. An officer spoke to him and he started at the voice as if his mind had been a long way off.

"I just stopped by after work," the woman in the blanket said to the man next to her, "to return her salad bowl. And the ambulance was here. How could this happen?" Without waiting for an answer, she clasped the blanket closed, turned, and tromped down the street and got into her car.

I tugged my hat down over my ears and retraced my steps down the block.

Ranger was waiting for me in the living room of the apartment I shared with my friend Gloria. He turned his head to look at me with his one eye, then jumped onto the back of the couch to wait for me to pet him. I smiled as he licked his white paw. That one white paw was the only reason Gloria had agreed to adopt him. She was superstitious about black cats.

The apartment smelled of radiator heat. Scant evening light reached between the buildings, mellowing the clash of our old, mismatched furniture. The room was the one thing that remained unchanged over the nine years since I'd graduated from the University of Indiana and arrived in Boston with a little

U-Haul and huge hopes.

Gloria wasn't home. I fed Ranger and ran a hot bath. While the water was running I glimpsed myself in the mirror. My normally wavy hair was limp and sticky with the humidity—like stretched strands of caramel. My lips looked pale and the zit on the side of my nose seemed angrier. The first few weeks of my new job were sanding me down.

I added some lavender and sea salt, but the bath didn't take my mind off of bodies on gurneys. I told myself the body on the street was a 102-year-old lady who had died peacefully. I told myself she hadn't died alone. I told myself she'd had children and grandchildren and that she'd told them stories of her life and passed on her recipes and knitting patterns. But the story I spun did nothing to settle my stomach. Maybe it was just the Indian food I'd had for dinner.

Gloria tripped into the apartment as I was getting a glass of water for bed. She giggled at her own clumsiness.

"You're in good spirits," I said.

"I went out with Anton. I didn't want to come home, but it was our first date. I don't want to look like a flooz."

I pressed my lips together to keep from commenting on her short skirt and four-inch heels. Gloria and I had been roommates for a long time and she was good at reading my thoughts.

"When are you going out again?"

"Tomorrow." She gave me an off-kilter smile, kicked off her shoes, and floated back to her bedroom.

Monday morning looked a lot like Sunday evening: Boston winter dim, and still months of it to go. I layered long underwear under charcoal slacks and pulled on a stretchy blue sweater. I wrangled my hair into a big clip and grabbed a granola bar on the way out the door. I was looking forward to a normal work day and forgetting about the body. I was ready to make it my best week in my new job.

Community Counseling Services rented space in a brick cube in South Boston not far from my apartment. Lynnie was on the phone at her desk in the reception area, where a musty institutional smell and molded plastic chairs were our clients' first introduction to us. "I'll work her in today at noon," Lynnie said, "and a visit to the Nayaks' at five thirty." Her eyes flicked to me and back to her ancient desktop computer. "No problem. Bye."

She hung up the phone and kept her eyes on the screen for a few beats before looking at me.

"No lunch for me? Is this an enforced diet or an emergency?"

"Oh, Penny, it's so sad—*really*," she said. "That was the Department of Children and Families. They need a counselor for a sixteen-year-old girl whose mom died yesterday. She's staying with her uncle." One hand was tugging at her short dark curls and she laid the other on her ample tummy. "My belly hurts. I should update my will. What would happen to my Tommy?"

Leave it to Lynnie to turn the situation around when I should be the one getting sympathy. My case load had started out heavy and had grown every week. I desperately needed time to get steady. My old job hadn't been easy, but I'd gained Weeble-Wobble status—the work could knock me over, but I wouldn't fall down. Now I felt more like Jenga —move one more piece and I'd collapse.

"No choice, no file, noon appointment." I did a little quarter turn on my heel and headed for my office. I made it about ten steps before my brain kicked into gear. I trotted back to the front. "When did you say she died? Was it near here?"

"Yesterday." She'd turned sullen. "The woman at DCF said they lived on Telegraph Hill. But the uncle's in Charlestown. Why?"

"I saw emergency vehicles on K Street last night on my way home from dinner," I said. "I assumed it was an old lady."

"Nope. It was some sort of accidental death, very sudden."

My stomach roiled. What were the chances that scene would come back to haunt me? But Southie was like a small town and we were the local social services agency, so, with our small staff, I guessed the chances were exactly one in four.

"Email me the uncle's address and I'll map directions. Routine home environment check, right?"

"Should be quick. You'll be in and out in a half hour."

At noon the girl, Dani Martin, appeared in my office doorway. I looked at her and paused. I would have guessed she was only fourteen. I saw her take in my office:

standard-issue old furniture to which I'd added a bright area rug, gem-colored pillows, and a collection of fidget toys on the coffee table.

"Dani, I'm Penny Wade," I said.

"What should I call you?" she asked with a frankness neither quite rude nor particularly polite.

"You can call me Penny." I swiveled my desk chair to face her as she walked into the office and sat on the old gray sofa. She tucked her feet up beside her.

"Okay, what next?" She took me in with huge dark eyes. She seemed resigned to endure an hour she would probably rather avoid.

"I expect you know that you were referred here by Family Services. I understand you lost your mom."

Her brown-gold eyes sparked. "I didn't lose her. She died. It's not like she lost her way on the T or something."

"No," I said, "it's not." I leaned forward, forearms on my knees, and studied her for a moment. Shiny dark hair framed her pretty oval face. I waited, gauged her. Despite the direct communication she looked incredibly vulnerable. "Dani, why don't you set the agenda? Tell me how you'd like to spend our time together."

"I want to find her murderer," she said.

"Murderer? I thought it was accidental."

"It couldn't have been," she said. "My mom was too careful. She never ate anything she wasn't sure about, and she always had an EpiPen."

"So she had a severe allergy?"

The look on her face said *duh* but she didn't say it out loud. "To tree nuts. But she was *always* careful. Even when she got an exposure she had an EpiPen—like a couple months ago, something was contaminated at a restaurant. She always tells them, but it's kind of scary, you know? If they don't clean the cutting board or something, she could get exposed. But she used an EpiPen and she was fine. That's only happened a couple of times."

"Did she use one last night?"

"The police said there wasn't one there. So I don't know for sure. It doesn't make sense."

She untucked her legs as she spoke and placed her low-cut black boots squarely on the floor. She leaned forward as if to get up, but she stayed. I saw the glint of a tear in her eye before she looked out the window at the misty sleet.

Grief and logic don't go hand-in-hand, but my job was to help her work through her irrational thoughts to a place of acceptance. When her eyes returned to me—intelligent, pained, but not pleading—I was ready to let her get everything out of her system. Then we could move on with her new reality. "Lay it on me," I said.

Dani described how she'd been in her high school's performance of *42nd Street* the previous night but her mom didn't show up. "Mom would never miss a performance," she said. "My Uncle Hank was there. He took me home. When we got there, there were all these cops on the street and an ambulance was pulling away." She stopped, swallowed hard. "Her boyfriend found her when he went to pick her up for my show. I just missed her. I didn't even get to see her." She stopped again and stared into the distance. I waited. She grabbed a pillow and hugged it in front of herself.

I waited. Finally she made eye contact.

"What happened next?" I asked—gentle voice.

"A cop drove me to my aunt and uncle's house in Charlestown. They asked me a lot of questions and I told them she would never make mistakes with her allergies but they didn't listen. They just treated me like a dumb kid." She looked at me like she was deciding whether I would do the same. "When they finally left, Aunt Josephine gave me a sedative and I went to sleep."

I made a mental note to ask who Hank was, if not her real uncle. "Dani, do you think someone would want to kill your mom?"

She answered with a shrug and a frown, "I don't know. She was great. I don't know why anyone would want to kill her. If I'd been there instead of at the stupid musical, this wouldn't have happened."

"No, Dani. Whenever you think of a way to blame yourself, I want you to hear my voice. It's normal to try to think of ways you could have prevented it, but you couldn't. It's not your fault."

She sat still, looking numb. She was clearly exhausted and probably hung over from whatever her aunt had given her. Her blank stare told me we needed to wrap up. "You know, we can talk more later. I'm going to be available to you if you need me, okay? You *will* find your way through this, and I'll help you." She looked at me with doe eyes and for a flash I saw what a persuasive young woman she could probably be when she wanted to. "Did you take the T here?" I asked.

She nodded.

"Is there someone at your aunt and uncle's house to be with you this afternoon?"

"No," she said, "but it's better like that, with them at work. I'll be fine." She started to stand but her first try failed. She'd sunk farther into the couch than she realized and she was out of energy. The lapse of grace didn't faze her and she got up. My heart panged because I had to let her go and she seemed so alone.

"Dani, I've been asked by Family Services to pay a visit to your aunt and uncle's house this evening. It's just routine because your mom's intentions for you aren't on record and they haven't reached your dad." I wanted to tread carefully on the dad question, since she hadn't mentioned him. "How do you feel about staying with your aunt and uncle?"

Dani sat on the arm of the couch, her arms heavy at her sides. Her eyes clouded over. "They're jerks," she said without inflection. "I hate them and their horrible house."

At five o'clock I left a marital affair, a minor theft, and Catholic guilt in their respective file folders and strode out of the office with printed directions in hand. I had on my trusty Uggs, the perfect choice for the cold wet streets I'd have to hike from the Community College T station to the Monument Square townhouse of Dob and Josephine Nayak.

The townhomes on Bunker Hill were graceful and well maintained. Even in December, the window boxes were beautifully decorated with holly, evergreens, and ornaments. In my neighborhood the window boxes had dead mums.

I was right on time. I have a knack for that. But by the time Mr. Nayak answered the doorbell I was four minutes late.

He opened the ridiculously big door and introduced himself. I told him my name, offered condolences, and accepted his outstretched hand. His fingers were thick and cold and his handshake too hard. He had the empty smile of a bumbling politician, but he'd just lost his sister, so I tried to let my judgments go.

I stepped into a white shiny foyer that smelled of floral air freshener. A ginger cat sprang over and began twining between my legs.

"They found it sitting next to her body, yowling," he said, "so I took it in too."

"What's his name?" I asked.

"She called him Peridot, for the eyes. Perry." As he spoke he reached down and grabbed the cat and tossed him out the still-open front door, then closed the door.

He waved me through the foyer into a cavernous formal living room. Also white. Heels clacked on the foyer tile, heralding Mrs.

Nayak. "You must be the social worker from Family Services," she said, extending her hand. "I'm Josephine Nayak, Dani's aunt." Her hand felt like baby powder. She had a long pale face and limp blond hair. I thought she was the woman I'd seen crying at the scene, but she was so made-up and composed that I couldn't be sure.

"Penny Wade," I said. "Thanks for making time."

Mr. Nayak cleared his throat and gestured toward an armchair. I crossed the thick carpet and took the seat. There was a white baby grand piano in the corner. My guess was that it was only for show.

"Please tell us how we can help you, Ms. Wade," he said, running his fingers over his five o'clock shadow. "Dani has stayed with us before and such formalities were never required." He remained standing. I couldn't tell whether he enjoyed the advantage or was just socially inept. Mrs. Nayak frowned at him and took a seat in a white chair across from me. I tried to hide a shiver. Was their heat on the fritz? They didn't seem to notice.

"Things are different with her mother gone," I said. "Until we hear from her father, she's a ward of the state, but I assure you this is routine."

Unless something substantial came to light, there was no reason to remove Dani from this house. It appeared clean and safe, and soulless décor wasn't a demerit on the home evaluation checklist. Mr. Nayak was pacing, Josephine was stiff and silent.

"Do you have an idea where her dad

might be?" I asked.

"We've told the police what we know," Mr. Nayak said. "It doesn't bear repeating with you." His words were flat.

I asked the required questions about Dani's care: transportation to school, support for getting on with her routine as soon as possible, those kinds of things, and Mrs. Nayak gave brief answers in a quiet voice.

"Mr. and Mrs. Nayak, is Dani here?"

There was a tense pause, then she said "yes" at the same moment he said "no." They turned their heads to glare at each other. Flames from their eyes threatened the brocade chairs.

"She was out with a friend," Mr. Nayak said. "Perhaps my wife is right and she's returned, but we need to spend some time as a family. She's had enough interrogation." Tension vibrated the air.

Mr. Nayak moved toward the door and Mrs. Nayak stood. I stood, walked back into the ice-palace foyer, and placed my card on a dainty French Provençal table there. I looked around but I didn't see any sign of Dani. "Thanks for your time. Family Services will be in touch with you soon."

The door shut quickly at my heel.

"*Oui, allo?*" my pal Toryn answered on the second ring.

"Hey, Toryn, it's Penny. Are you eating snails or sipping pinot gris?" I'd poured a glass of Malbec when I got home from the Nayaks' and sat on a stool at our black tile breakfast bar. The wine was round and dry.

"Both, of course, chou-chou."

Ugh, he took it too far, but I smiled despite myself. "I'm calling with a favor." I needed help and my inside line to the DA's office might be just the ticket. "It's about a woman who died in my neighborhood last night. Anita Martin." I recapped what I knew.

"Sad, sad, sad," he said. I could picture him in his South End studio, probably at the big window by the balcony. He was long and lean with an oversized head and wild hair. Kind of a curly paintbrush of a guy.

"I can't tell you this, of course," I said, "but I have her daughter as a new client. I want to help her get some closure, but she has a lot of questions about what happened. Any chance you could get a look at the file and see what the medical examiner said?" Even as I said it, I didn't know why I was asking. The cause of death was known. But there were the nagging questions of how she got exposed, and whether the EpiPen had failed, or if there was one at all.

"I should spend an unauthorized snoop chip on this? It doesn't sound that fascinating."

"*Please*, I feel like a total failure at my new job so far and I just want to help *someone*. If you could see her even your crystalline heart might crack."

Toryn and I agreed to meet for dinner the following evening. I was too tired to make a meal, so after staring at a jug of iced tea and a half head of dead broccoli in the fridge, I slapped some peanut butter on a piece of bread, folded it over, and took my laptop to my bed. Ranger hopped up and tried to climb onto the keyboard.

I didn't find much about Anita on the internet, just a LinkedIn profile with a head shot. She had the same clear oval face as Dani, with skin a shade darker. According to her profile on LinkedIn, she'd graduated from Lesley University in 1995 with a degree in design. She worked at Mt. Vernon Jewelers on Beacon Hill as a designer.

I showered but I couldn't go to sleep even after I made up my mind that I'd let my curiosity go far enough. Social work is vulnerable to scope creep. The trick is to keep focused on a realistic objective: in this case, to help Dani process what had happened and find closure. I sent up a prayer that Toryn would find something to settle Dani's mind about her mom's death, and then I could do my job. I needed my job.

CHAPTER TWO

On Tuesday, my office phone rang at 10 a.m. as I was waiting for a transsexual client who had changed her mind when she realized how much gender advantage she'd lost when she became a woman.

It was Dani. "I found your card after you left last night," she said. "Oh—this is Dani Martin. Is it okay that I called?"

"Yes, Dani, it is," I said, glad to hear her voice. "How are you?"

"Um. Okay, I guess. I—well, I don't know if you can help. Maybe it's stupid of me to call." Her voice was uneven. "I want to go home," she said. "My aunt and uncle are at work, and I don't want to go alone. I just need some stuff and I want to be there for a few minutes. I know she won't be there, but maybe I can feel her or smell her or… you probably think I'm crazy."

"No, Dani. I get it," I said, trying to think fast. It was her house and of course she had a key—which ethical prohibition was I supposed to be remembering? "It just seems like something your family should do with you."

"They won't." I heard her voice shutting down. I was about to be one more adult who treated her like a child and left her with nobody she could trust to help her. I was in a tight spot.

"Uh, I have two more clients before a lunch break at noon. Do you want to come by here at noon and we'll figure it out together?"

"Oh, thank you, Penny! Yes. Thank you." She hung up.

I hadn't meant to commit, but I was having trouble saying no to Dani. I knew what it was like to spend every day with someone you expected would always be there and then suddenly be without her.

Lynnie gave me a long questioning blink when I met Dani in the lobby and the two of us walked past her desk. We turned down West Broadway and were halfway down the block, both staring at our shoes, when Dani spoke.

"I don't want to believe it's real. Maybe we shouldn't go because I kind of expect to see her there."

"Do you want to get a cup of coffee first and talk about what to do?" I hoped she would change her mind because I still felt like I was breaking some rule I couldn't put my finger on.

Dani had stepped out of the sidewalk traffic and paused. I stopped next to her and dug in my bag for my cell phone while I waited for her decision. I had the feeling I would need more than an hour in any case.

"Okay," she said, looking up at me, "where?"

"There's that funky place around the corner. They have great scones."

We ordered at the counter and settled into a tiny table against a wall of local artists' paintings. Dani had a cinnamon scone and a cup of vanilla-flavored coffee into which she'd dumped a bunch of cream. I remembered the days when extra pounds didn't call for a decision between cream and a scone. I had black tea and nothing. I claim virtue where I can. I made a quick call to Lynnie.

"Is it okay to cancel a meeting?" Dani asked when I was off the phone. "Is someone gonna bust or something because you weren't there?"

"It's fine," I said. "In fact, this client will probably be relieved to have the session canceled." I crossed my fingers under the table in a wish that my client was doing okay that week. I wondered what my boss, Vivian, would say. I was screwing up already. "Dani, let's talk about why you want to go back to the apartment today, and why not. What would you like to do there?"

Her eyes were guarded and she had her arms crossed. "I mostly just want my stuff," she said.

The path was slippery. I looked at my mug, trying not to make her feel scrutinized. I wished I had a scone to pick at. "Sure, I can understand that. Anything else?" I willed myself to wait patiently. Why were my counseling skills going out the window with this girl? *Wait… wait… wait…* I chanted to myself.

Nothing.

"Would you like to arrange to have someone pick up your stuff for you? Then you wouldn't have to go."

She shifted in her seat and unfolded her arms to take a sip of coffee. She poked at the scone. "No. They wouldn't get the right stuff," she said, "and I just want to be there a little. Everyone acts like I should just move on and forget my whole life so far."

Life from zero to sixteen, pretty much the section I'd forgotten. But I guess I hadn't forgotten it yet at her age. "I don't think you should forget any of it, Dani. A lot of times it helps to write about memories. Some people make photo collages of their loved ones for the memorial service. Do you have a lot of pictures?"

"I don't know," she said, "I guess, but only since I've had my phone. I know where some boxes of Mom's old photos are though. I should get them."

We sat in silence for a few minutes. Dani ate her scone. I sipped tea and worried about what was next. If we didn't go, I was afraid Dani wouldn't have access to whatever she needed to get closure. If we went, I didn't know exactly what I was worried about, but I felt my stomach tightening.

When she'd finished her scone, Dani pulled a Smurfette keychain out of her pocket and dangled it between us on one finger. She swung her head in the direction of the door and stood. *All righty then*, I thought.

It was a ground floor apartment with a small stonework balcony overlooking the street. The front door opened into the living room. It smelled empty. No lingering coffee or perfume, no baking or laundry.

Vibrant traditional Indian fabrics covered the pillows and there was a crimson Indian area rug that seemed to glow from within. I walked over and touched a throw that was folded over the back of an armchair. It had rich shades of red and orange, threaded with gold.

"My grandpa was from Jaipur," Dani said. "He had a shop with stuff from India."

Dani turned left into the kitchen and opened a top drawer. "Look—no EpiPens. They're always here."

She checked the other drawers. No EpiPens. She pushed the button on the answering machine. Three messages from Sunday. There was a reminder from the pharmacy that Anita's prescription was ready, a message from someone named Jill inviting Anita to a cocktail get-together Friday evening, and a message from a man saying he'd pick her up in a half hour. I assumed that was the boyfriend who found her, but didn't want to ask Dani.

Dani took a deep breath, opened a lower cabinet, and found a couple of cloth grocery bags. She headed for her bedroom. I followed and sat on the purple spread of her single bed, remembering my own childhood room, my own pink spread, stained with magic markers and tears. Dani pulled clothes from her closet and started shoving them into the bags.

"Let me fold," I said. She dumped the clothes on her bed and moved to her little wooden desk while I folded jeans, leggings, tunics, and T-shirts, mostly in shades of blue, purple, and black. She added a stuffed unicorn, a carved wooden angel, a seashell, and a stack of CDs to the bag, then practically tiptoed into her mother's room. I followed.

Anita's bed was made, though not neatly, with a red and pink silky spread. A few clothes were strewn around on the hardwood floor. Novels and jewelry industry magazines were piled on the floor by the bed, adding a bookish smell to the stale air.

Dani took a glass-framed photo off Anita's dresser. Over her shoulder I saw mother and daughter laughing and playing in the fountains on the Common. Dani must have been five or six. The two looked strikingly similar and very, very happy. Also on the dresser was a picture of a couple in about their late forties, an Indian man with a white woman. "Your grandparents?" I asked.

"Yep, my grandma died before I was born. Grandpa moved here when he was in his twenties and met my grandma. I guess it was a big deal for her to marry an Indian man. How dumb is that?" She gestured to the third frame. "That's Mom's boyfriend, Brian." He was handsome if a little tweedy: a close-cropped beard starting to gray, intense dark blue eyes, wire-rimmed glasses. I recognized him as the man standing by the ambulance on the receiving end of the sobbing woman's stare the night Anita died.

Dani opened her mom's second drawer. She dug behind socks and pantyhose and pulled out three small boxes. She opened them to reveal three pieces of jewelry. Dani took one out and explained that it was called a *maang tikka*, a kind of hair jewelry. She demonstrated how someone would wear it with the long string of little diamonds down a middle part in her hair and the tear-shaped ruby resting on her forehead. "These probably aren't real," she told me, and put the *maang tikka*, a string of pearls, and a man's ring into their boxes and put them in one of her bags.

I didn't like being at the back of the apartment. I didn't want to make Dani nervous, and I didn't want her to think I believed there was a murderer on the loose, but my skin felt chilly and my ears were all but bending toward the front door.

Dani walked over and opened the bedside table drawer. "EpiPens," she said. "See? She always kept them around. Maybe she couldn't get here in time." Her eyes filled with tears and I knew she was imagining the scene. I also knew that she would imagine the worst. I didn't want her to get stuck in the made-up images. Healing means processing the past and moving to now.
I needed to help Dani get closure and set a healthy path forward. Which reminded me...

"Do you want to get the pictures you mentioned and make a collage or a slide show for the service?"

Dani nodded and went to her mom's walk-in closet. Next to Anita's professional clothes, T-shirts, and jeans was a section of bright-colored saris. Dani ran her fingers down the silk of a sapphire-blue one.

"When my mom was little they'd visit her grandparents in India. She wanted to be an Indian princess. Her grandpa had a gem-processing facility in Jaipur so she grew up loving gems. But it was dangerous back then. One of her uncles was killed over something to do with gems." She pulled a pomegranate-seed-red sari from its hanger and handed it to me. I folded it and put it in a bag. "What will happen to all her stuff?" she asked.

"I guess you and your uncle will sort through and box up whatever you want to keep."

She nodded and knelt down by a low shelf of shoes and shoe boxes. She chose a box and opened it—photos. I glimpsed a yellowed photo of a dark-haired little boy and wondered if he had turned into gigantic Dob. She replaced the top and reached for another box. Shoes. A few more tries produced more shoes and some belts and scarves. While she searched boxes I stepped out into the hallway to reassure myself that no one else was in the apartment. Everything looked okay but there were noises in the outer hallway and my hair pricked a little. I wanted to get Dani out of there. When I went back to the bedroom Dani was in the middle of a mess of shoe boxes, plastic storage containers, and shopping bags.

"She had some pieces of jewelry that she kept really hidden. I saw them a couple of times, but I don't know where she hid them."

"I'm sure you'll find them when you go through everything later," I said.

Just then we heard the front door lock click and the door open. We looked at each other and froze. We heard shuffling noises in the living room. We stayed, kneeling on the closet floor. We listened to cabinet doors banging, and then steps coming down the hallway. I glanced around, hoping for a baseball bat, a tire iron, or a cast iron pan. I grabbed the spikiest high heel I could find. Dani's face drained of color and she squeezed her eyes shut. I thought she would scream but then we heard the bathroom door shut and the sound of a man peeing. Who breaks into a house and uses the bathroom? We heard the toilet flush and the sink running. Seconds later a man's figure appeared backlit in the bedroom doorway.

"Dani?"

She didn't speak.

"It's me, Brian."

He stepped through the room and into the closet with us. I stood and extended my hand before realizing I was still holding the shoe. I chucked it aside, then hoped the toss didn't look too careless—what if it was their first date shoe or something?

"Hi, I'm Penny Wade. I'm a counselor at Community Counseling Services down the street." I paused, unsure how to explain how that role had landed me in his dead girlfriend's closet.

"Penny came with me so I could get some stuff," Dani said.

I smiled with relief but tried to make it look casual and friendly.

"Brian," Dani said, "I looked for EpiPens in the kitchen and didn't find any. When you found her was it—was she..." Her voice cracked.

"It was too late when I got here, Dani. I'm sorry. And I have no idea why she didn't have an EpiPen. I wondered the same thing, of course."

He looked uncomfortable and I was starting to sweat. I wanted out of the close quarters of the closet but he was in the doorway, shifting from foot to foot.

"I needed to pick up some of my stuff too," he said. He took half a step toward Dani then seemed to think better of it in the small space. "How are..." he paused, "I mean, is there anything, well, you need?" He glanced at the floor and back at her. "Uh, that I can do?"

"I'm okay." She fiddled with the box of photos and glanced out of the closet over his shoulder. "Thanks, though, I'll let you know if I need something."

I thought he should offer to give Dani his key, but he didn't. He took off his glasses and cleaned them with his untucked shirt. He put them back on and looked at Anita's saris hanging next to him. He reached out as if to touch them, then turned and left the room.

When Brian and Dani had gathered their stuff, they said an awkward goodbye. When he was gone we turned off the lights, locked up, and left.

Dani thanked me, slung her bags over her shoulders, and headed back to the T.

When I reached the office I passed Lynnie quickly while she was tied up checking someone out. I would answer her questions later.

My hawkish boss, Vivian, was out of the office. My agency mentor, Nathan, was there and I was glad I would have some privacy to tell him about Dani. I'd learned that this kind of work required support, which was part of why I took the job with Vivian, Nathan, and Lynnie. Unfortunately, my first impressions of Vivian were not spot on—she wasn't a bad person, and was probably a good therapist, but she was a micro-manager and harsh. Nathan was a family therapist and a hero. He had been active in civil rights in the South when it was dangerous for African-American men to do anything in the South.

"Nathan?" I poked my head into his open door. "Are you waiting for a client?"

When he turned toward me I saw today's nature-scene sweatshirt—songbirds on an evergreen branch.

"Yes and no," he said. "I think he's a no-show. Come on in."

I closed the door behind me and sat in the straight chair next to his gray metal desk. Nathan leaned back in his chair and waited. From the moment we met at my job interview, I'd felt like he could be the life vest under the airplane seat—unobtrusive, but there if I needed him. In social work, mentors can take roles helping with professional duties, but also serve in a more personal counseling capacity to help the mentee to deal with stresses of the job which, in an emotional business like ours, often overlap with personal issues. It's a pretty broad job description, and in our case, Nathan did whatever he thought would help me navigate the job and stay sane.

When I thought I was ready to speak I tried, but found my throat had tightened, so I waited some more and Nathan waited with me.

Finally I squeaked out, "New client. Mom died. Good mom..."

"Tell me," he said, and I found his voice and the faint peppermint smell in his office soothing. I managed to bring him up to date without mentioning our expedition to Anita's apartment.

"Penny, what's the hardest thing about working with Dani?"

Damn. He was going to turn this conversation to me. But he was right. I'd worked with kids who lost a parent before, but this one was much more emotional. "It's just that she loved her mom and her mom loved her and her dad is nowhere and now..." I squashed some sobs.

Nathan handed me tissues. "Will sixteen years with love from one parent be enough?" I asked. "Will she be able to love a good man? Be a good mom?" I felt uncomfortably transparent under Nathan's gaze. I thought about my own mom, who would send me to my room if I cried for any reason. She didn't want to hear it, so she solved her problem without ever considering mine.

"I can't answer about Dani," he said, "but people from all kinds of circumstances manage those things quite well. And people from seemingly good homes botch it all up. I think it's as much about the individual as their upbringing."

I thought about that, for myself and for Dani. I thought her chances seemed pretty good, but we had to get her through her questions about her mom's death.

"I want to tell you one story," Nathan

said. "It's about a client I had nearly two decades ago, a young man who was gay, but closeted. Jeffrey was terrified of how his friends and family would react if he came out, and he started dealing with his discomfort by doing drugs. At first he smoked pot and drank, then after a while that wasn't enough and he moved on to other drugs—maybe coke, I don't remember exactly."

I watched him as he looked from me to the ceiling and back, pulling the memory from long ago, imparting it on me.

"There was something about him that tugged at me. I spent a lot of time thinking of how to help him and I tried to create ways to move him away from his new drug-using friends. I took his phone calls during off-hours, I even met him for dinner when he really needed someone. I wanted him to see what it was like to be around someone who accepted him for who he was."

He took a deep breath, looked up at the ceiling again, and pulled down the final chunk of memory. "I helped too much. Or, I should say, I didn't help at all. He thought he had fallen in love with me and I had to end our counseling relationship. It was a mess. My agency fired me, and worse than that, I failed him."

I muddled through my last two client sessions, distracted and cursing myself for making dinner arrangements with Toryn. I wanted to go home and curl up in bed. But I was also curious about what he'd found.

When I arrived at the Thai place, Toryn

had snagged a table so we got our food and dug in. The peanutty noodles were good, if a bit on the heavy side. I squeezed some lime juice on them.

The walk over had given me some energy and I was feeling better. Part of me didn't want to talk about the Dani thing. Maybe we could just chit-chat. I could hear about his boyfriend and he could ask about my nonexistent love life, a regular Toryn and Penny evening.

"I have some info on the body," he said, interrupting my escape planning.

I saw two heads jerk up at the table behind Toryn. Crap. This was a bad idea.

"College students eavesdropping six o'clock," I whispered.

Toryn leaned in. "It was anaphylaxis. She'd ingested tree nuts in a cheese Danish. Was fairly quick. She had dragged herself through her vomit, though, so it wasn't instantaneous."

I looked at my peanutty noodles and set my chopsticks down.

The college students were still tuned in. Two women got up from a table by the window and I swung my head in that direction, raising my eyebrows at Toryn. With one sweeping motion he was up, with his pad Thai in one hand and his water and chopsticks in the other. I shot the students a smug look as we left.

Seated again, I asked, "Was there an EpiPen there? Did she use one?"

"No EpiPen."

I was always amazed at the level of

detail he could get as an administrative assistant at the DA, but then again, who has more information than admins? "Dani says she always had EpiPens on hand. She sees this as proof that Anita's death wasn't an accident."

"Maybe she ran out of them," he said.

"It's not like people just go through those like tissue. Besides, she had some by her bed."

"I don't know, Penny," Toryn said. "The girl is grieving. She's in denial. You must deal with the grieving process with clients all the time. She's gonna have to accept what's happened."

Shame-heat warmed my face. I hadn't meant to sound like I thought it was murder. I just wanted something to reassure Dani. Still, something was nagging at the back of my mind and I couldn't dismiss Dani's fears until I could convince her it was an accident.

"I see you're siding with the police," I snapped. "That's a switch for you. You usually go on about their incompetence."

"Look, Penny, there's something personal about this for you and I think it's muddling things up a little. Do you see yourself in her?"

"No!" It came out kind of loud and heads turned our way. I controlled my voice. "I should be so lucky."

"To have your mom die?" he asked.

"She's dead anyway," I began, hoping to make sense of this before more came out of my mouth. "But no, to have a mom who was a good mom before she died." I was angry with Toryn for drawing me out, and tears gathered in the corners of my eyes. "I've gotta go. I don't need this shit from you." I signed the credit card slip and stood up.

Toryn swung his bowed head from side to side. His long neck made the gesture especially dramatic. "Redheads," he muttered.

My face got even hotter. He knew how much I hated that. I'm not a redhead. "I'm outta here." I stomped out as dramatically as I could in my rubber-bottomed boots. I couldn't make much clomping noise, but I managed a few squeaks on the tile floor.

CHAPTER THREE

"Uncle Dob reached Chris—my dad. I guess he'd been in the Catskills out of cell range." Dani was in my office for her scheduled session on Wednesday morning. "He's coming here and he wants me to go back to Philly with him and his freaky wife." She was curled up on the couch. Her hair was in a doubled-over ponytail and her expression was similarly no-nonsense.

She twisted a hair scrunchie around her fingers as she spoke. "The lawyer read the will. Mom named Uncle Dob the executor. Nobody told me how much money is in there, but Mom had an inheritance from her dad." Dani made occasional eye contact with me but mostly stared at the scrunchie. "They scheduled the funeral for Saturday."

"Wow, Dani, that's a lot. How do you feel about seeing your dad?"

"It's been a long time, maybe a year. He's never shown much interest—new life now and all. I don't want to leave here and have to live in Philly."

Dani got up and walked to the window. I moved from my desk chair to a straight chair across from the couch. I picked up some magnetic fidget balls and fiddled with them.

"I have a friend with connections to the police," I said. "I asked him to look at your mom's file. I'm not sure if anyone will have told you what the medical examiner found."

She turned and went back to her seat on the couch. She sat up straight and pressed her fists into the cushion at her sides.

"They confirmed that she died by anaphylaxis. There was a significant amount of tree nut contamination in an undigested pastry. She didn't use an EpiPen. She didn't suffer—it was quick." I took a deep breath.

She was silent for a few beats.

"How do they think she'd eat something with nuts? And how do they explain the missing EpiPens? There were none in her purse, the kitchen, the living room! Do they think she was stupid?" She began to cry.

My psychology training started yakking in my head: *This is good, she's moving from denial to grief and acceptance. The airing of unanswered questions is cathartic. It's painful, but it's progress.*

I handed her a tissue box and let her cry.

When her crying died down I changed the subject. I needed to know how she was getting along in the ice castle. "Tell me about staying with your aunt and uncle. Is it going okay so far?"

"I don't have much choice, do I?"

I waited. She slid her scrunchie over her wrist and picked up a rubber twisty toy horse from the table and torqued its legs around.

"I have a room on the third floor, so at least I'm away from them. I can burn candles and stuff and they don't know because they're too lazy to walk up there. They just yell when they want something."

"Is your room nice?" I prompted.

"It's okay, but I feel like a prisoner. Dob says we have to be frugal with my trust fund, so he's only giving me twenty dollars in spending money each week and he canceled my voice lessons. I really loved my voice lessons. Dob's a jerk."

"What about Josephine?"

"She doesn't want me there. I don't mind doing chores and stuff but she makes me feel like I'm doing them to earn the right to stay there."

"That sounds really uncomfortable, Dani."

"They're hardly ever there and when they are they argue with each other and ignore me."

I felt a familiar hollowness. I knew what it was like to grow up in a house like that. "Dani, you have sixteen years of your mother's love inside you. It'll give you strength. We'll work together to get you through this."

She bit her lip and looked at my clock. "Gotta go." As she stood she said, "I want to show you something. Will you meet me at Mount Vernon Jewelers on Beacon Hill later? What time do you get off work?"

"I finish at five," I heard myself saying. She probably just wanted someone to hear about her mom—memories and stuff—and see her jewelry. We were moving in the right direction.

After work I took the T to the Charles MGH station and walked down Charles to Mt. Vernon Street and Mt. Vernon Jewelers. A wind chime jingled when I opened the door and I stepped in quickly to keep the cold out. Dani was there with a grandfatherly man who reminded me of Captain Kangaroo. He rose to greet me.

"I'm Harry. It's a pleasure to meet you. I'm sorry the circumstances aren't better. Please come in and sit. I've made tea."

He had a British accent and warm eyes. His shop was inviting in an old-world way, with red velvet upholstered chairs grouped for conversation and low tables for tea.

I sat in a chair by Dani, who gave me a half smile. "I wanted to show you how Mom had EpiPens everywhere, but Harry can tell you, and how careful she was too."

"Dani speaks the truth," Harry said. "Anita was highly cautious, as was called for by her situation. She kept EpiPens in the drawer by the register, in her desk, and in her handbag. She always did her research too. Restaurants, processed foods. What a lot of trouble to have to worry whether your porridge was processed in a factory with pecans."

So much for progress toward acceptance. "I don't know what good it does for you to convince me, Dani. I'm not the police and I don't know how to answer your unanswered questions."

"You have to believe me! Someone killed her. You believe me, don't you, Harry?"

Harry's brow creased. He fidgeted with

the cream and sugar on the tea tray. Finally under Dani's hot stare he said, "Oh, now, Dani, I'm sure I'm not qualified to say. I don't imagine they can prove it one way or another, can they." It was more of a statement than a question. The English are masters of the hybrid.

Dani crossed her arms and Harry changed the subject. "Penny, Dani's been like a grandchild to me, Anita was the daughter I never had." He reached for Dani's hand and she uncrossed her arms and gave it to him. "I have sons, three of them. None have Anita's aptitude for the jewelry business and only one has any interest. I had hoped Anita would run the shop when I retire. I can't imagine what I'll do without her. She was the heart of this place: a gifted designer, adored by our customers, and always working to make the world a little better."

He reached behind him and took three brochures from holders on the counter. He set them in front of me. "We specialize in fair-trade gems and precious metals. It was her idea. There's a good market for responsibly sourced jewelry, especially around here." He circled his hand in the air. "Her designs, of course, also made us popular. Can I show you a few of her pieces?"

I glanced at Dani, who was comfortably curled in her chair with her tea in her hands. I imagined her spending afternoons here after school, watching Harry and Anita work.

"I'd love to see them."

Harry rose and went to a display case. He arranged three pieces on a black velvet board and returned to his seat.

There was a *maang tikka*, this one with elaborate curling designs in gold that would be pinned in a woman's hair and a central ruby over a fringe of teardrop-shaped pearls that would rest on her forehead. There was a very simple ring, a pink stone set in platinum.

"What is this?" I asked.

"Sapphire," Harry said with a smile. "A pink sapphire. Did you know that rubies and sapphires come from the same mineral? It's called corundum—aluminum oxide. The presence of small amounts of other minerals are responsible for the color. Rubies are made red by chromium, and sapphires blue from titanium and iron, but sapphires can be different colors too, like this one."

The third piece was a gold bracelet with intricate scrolling designs punctuated by small inlaid rubies. I'm not much of a jewelry person, but Anita's pieces seemed to have soul. "They're lovely," was all I managed to say.

"She especially loved rubies," Harry said. "They have such interesting tales associated with them, in addition to their extraordinary beauty."

Dani had a faint smile on her face as she listened to Harry. It appeared to be a comfortable pattern for them. I wanted to make it last.

Harry didn't need encouragement. He slid shortbread cookies out of a plastic sleeve onto a plate between us. Dani took one and nibbled. Harry continued, "Rubies represent the love and passion deep within each of us.

One Indian legend says that rubies were born of the blood of a demon." He paused and leaned toward Dani. "Love and beauty are tempered by many forces."

"Tell Penny about the Emperor in the painting," Dani said, pointing to what looked like a black and white etching print behind the counter.

"Ah, the Emperor, well, you see, Burma was a land of great rubies. They found their way out of rocks by tumbling down rivers. One day a peasant found a ruby the size of a hen's egg in the river and took it to the Emperor to show his love for his leader and his land. The Emperor put the ruby in a glass of milk and the ruby turned the milk red."

He noticed my puzzled expression and nodded. "I think it's the kind of story where you supply your own interpretation," he said.

Harry had distracted Dani from her worries and comforted her in the cocoon of the shop and his stories. He glanced at her. "Your mother came back from India with wonderful stories. You know Jaipur is divided into nine districts to represent the nine planets, nine signs of the zodiac. Each sign of the zodiac is associated with its own gem.

"The Nayaks are an old and distinguished family in Jaipur," he continued, "did you know that, my dear? You have a fascinating heritage. Anita was energized when she returned from her last trip. The connection with her childhood memories and her family's past must have refueled her. That, and her family treated her like a princess." He winked at Dani. "You know, she sent me a card when she was there. Would you like me to read it?"

"Yes! Please." She stirred in her seat and set her cup down.

Harry got up and returned the jewelry to its case and locked the case. He went behind the counter to his desk and retrieved the card. He read it out loud when he returned to his seat.

Dear Harry,

It was a long trip here but I've arrived and am being well looked after by my cousin Leena and her family. They live in a beautiful home on a hillside overlooking Jaipur. They took me to the City Palace at the center of Old Town. It's now an amazing museum full of artifacts. Such interesting architecture, gardens and courtyards! I couldn't absorb it all. This card shows the "Hall of Public Audience," but doesn't begin to represent the intricate detail of the architecture! I plan to visit the gem processing facility tomorrow. I'll have so much to tell you when I get home!

Much love to you,
Anita

"It's not a long note, but I thought you'd like it. You may keep it if you like, Dani."

Dani was still for a moment, then took the card, stood, and thanked Harry with a hug. She turned to me. "It's almost six thirty," she said, "we should go."

"I'm glad of your visit, my girl, and pleased to have made your acquaintance, Penny. Come back any time." He turned to Dani and touched her arm. "Dani, call me if you need anything. I'll see you Saturday at the least."

Dani hugged him again and turned to go, but she turned back. "I almost forgot, do you have Brian's cell phone number? I tried to email him but I got an out-of-office reply that said he's traveling. I want to make sure he knows about the service."

"I'm sorry, I don't, my dear. I checked your mom's Rolodex myself, I was going to call with condolences. I imagine he's learned about the service though, I'm sure we'll see him then."

Dani and I walked up Charles Street past upscale boutiques and restaurants, many with side doors leading to overpriced studio apartments above. We were headed to the Charles MGH T station. We both needed the red line, though Dani would only go two stops and switch to the orange line to Charlestown. As we walked up the hill Dani fiddled with the toggles on her jacket.

"There's something I haven't told you," she said. "I don't want my mom to be in any trouble and I just thought, well, I shouldn't say anything, but—"

"It's okay. What you say to me is confidential unless you and I agree otherwise."

"It's just that she seemed really weird the last few weeks."

"Weird how?"

"She'd lose her temper more often, like she was really edgy all the time. She would fight with Brian and snap at me and stuff."

Had Dani been reading detective novels to figure out how to raise suspicion or something? I mean, as much as I hated to doubt her, she was definitely working the angles to make me believe her mom had been murdered.

She continued, "When I asked her about it she said it was nothing, just stress. But I know there was something going on. I could hear her cry sometimes at night and she looked tired and didn't eat much—even when I made her banana pancakes." Her voice cracked a little.

"I'm so sorry. I can see it's weighing on you, but it isn't necessarily a sign that something was terribly wrong. People go through hard emotional times for lots of reasons."

We reached the top of the hill and I offered to buy her dinner at The King and I. I could tell she dreaded going back to the Nayaks' house and I always had a very hard time walking past The King and I. She accepted. She pulled out her phone and left a message for Josephine, then sent a couple of texts.

No matter how much great food they have on that menu, I could never break away from the tofu pad Thai. It's the best comfort food in Boston. Dani ordered a Thai iced tea and some vegetable rolls.

I drew her out enough to get her to talk a little about regular teen stuff. She half hid behind her hair while she quietly told me a little about the cliques in high school, how stupid most of the boys were, and about her favorite classes—art and theater.

"I want to go to a performing arts

college, then go to New York or LA," she said. "I love stage acting but I don't know much about film yet." The more she talked the more animated she became. "My voice teacher says I have the talent for musicals. He got to perform on Broadway!" Dani had a full-blown smile on her face, the first I'd seen.

Somehow I agreed to drive her out to Wayland to see Uncle Hank, the friend who had driven her home from the musical the night her mom died. I was definitely getting more involved than the therapeutic guidelines might suggest.

We drove up to Wayland Thursday morning in a red Prius I'd rented from Zipcar on West Broadway. Dani explained that Hank was her grandpa's best friend. He was a retired police chief and Aunt Jenny a retired nurse practitioner.

Their house was a mid-century modern home in a well-off neighborhood. I didn't like well-off suburban neighborhoods. I grew up in one. It was sidewalkless, soulless, and the lack of community handicapped me for life. Well, having lousy parents didn't help either.

But Hank and Jenny's house was surprisingly cozy inside. We sat in the sunny kitchen, where Hank served dark coffee with an undertone of cinnamon, and fresh lemon muffins. I'd called in sick to work and felt all the more guilty for enjoying myself. When pleasantries were finished, Dani dove right into her agenda.

"Uncle Hank, I don't think Mom died by mistake. I want to tell you why so you can help me."

Jenny squinted slightly and tilted her head. The lines by her eyes described a lifetime of smiles. Uncle Hank's eyebrows shot up and he focused on Dani. He put his elbows on the table and leaned toward her. "Okay, Dani," he said. "I'm sure the police had reasons for their conclusions, but tell us what concerns you."

Dani explained the missing EpiPens and her mom's recent edginess, adding that she had called the pharmacy the previous evening to see if the waiting prescription was EpiPens. It was just birth control pills.

I couldn't read Hank or Jenny and I suspected they were keeping careful control of their reactions so as not to either encourage or discourage Dani. I wondered which.

Jenny spoke first. "I have to agree that it's unusual that Anita would find herself without an EpiPen. But darling, I don't think anyone would harm her intentionally."

"I agree with Jenny," Hank added, nodding his balding gray head.

He sat back in his chair and took a sip of coffee. Dani shifted and tucked one foot under her on her chair.

I held my breath. Hank and Jenny's opinion might sway Dani to give up on the murder thing.

"There may be a simple explanation," Hank said. "A missing EpiPen certainly doesn't make for murder." He paused. "We'll probably never know what was bothering your mom, but the fact that she was moody is no reason for suspicion either."

Jenny nodded and got up to refill our coffees. I hoped Hank would be completely clear that he would help prove that it was just an accident.

He continued, "Let me make some calls and see what I can learn. We know it was ruled an accidental death by the police, and I won't claim we're infallible, but they must have had a reason."

On Friday I arrived at the office early and optimistic. I was sure that with Hank and Jenny's help, Dani would soon put her suspicions behind her. I knew I could help her move through her grief and gain some confidence and independence.

I tidied up my office, deleted junk emails, and triaged the ones that weren't junk. Before my first client, I stopped in the bathroom to try to tame my hair, which is inconveniently between wavy and curly. In some ways that's okay though, because I can cultivate that "it's out of my control" impression.

When I came out of the ladies' room I looked up to see the gigantic back of Dob Nayak loping toward my office.

"Mr. Nayak, how can I help you?" I glanced down the hall to see if Nathan's door was open. It wasn't.

Dob turned. I didn't like the bow of his head nor his lowered brow. In four long strides, he stepped very close to me and looked straight down. I'm pretty tall, but he had a good six inches on me.

"I've come to ask you to please stay out

of my family's affairs. Dani is confused and grieving. You are encouraging her imagination. It will be best for her if you remove yourself from the situation. If you don't I'll speak to your supervisor." Even in a threat the guy was kind of bumbling; his speech was overly formal and he seemed awkward in that big body. Should I be terrified or was he just muddling his way through his grief and trying to simplify things and sort them out?

"I've been retained by Family Services to help Dani to process her mother's death, and that is my only goal." I sounded pretty good considering he was towering so close I could feel his hot breath. "I assure you I'm not encouraging anything other than healthy progress through the grieving process."

His face reddened a shade and he pulled himself up even taller. I smelled sharp cologne. Sweat pricked my armpits.

"We don't agree, Ms. Wade." He drew out the "Ms." the way men do when they think women should be clearly labeled "Miss" or "Mrs." "I expect you to bring immediate closure to your relationship with Dani. I assure you it will be the best for everyone."

He turned and strode back down the hall and out the door. I wiped my palms on my slacks and reminded myself to breathe.

CHAPTER FOUR

I had to promise to clean the bathroom for a month, but I convinced Gloria to go to the funeral with me.

At first she'd shaken her gigantic kinky hair and said, "Penny, funerals in the US are the worst. Everyone is bottled up and bitter."

"Please, Gloria, I don't want to go alone."

"There'll be people there. Protestant people? Is it a Protestant funeral?"

"I don't know, I guess so. What's wrong with that?"

Gloria threw up her hands and looked to the sky. "Mexican families, we show our grief. We let it out for God to see. When my *abuela* died, we cried and moaned for nine days, saying the rosary and taking candles to the altar every day."

"Then aren't Protestant funerals easier?"

"No, I think you'll all die of cancer, keeping your feelings inside like that."

But I'd made my promise and she gave in.

"*Dios mio*, Penny. The things I do for you!"

The service was in Charlestown. Gloria and I were greeted inside the stone church's dim foyer by a gentleman who smiled kindly and handed us programs. We walked into the church, breathing the smell of death lilies. I saw the back of Dani's head in the front row. I wished I could let her know I was there, but I wasn't going near Dob Nayak. Gloria and I found a seat midway back on the left and watched mourners file in. Everyone I'd met so far had arrived before us and sat up front. Dob and Josephine sat on Dani's right, and I guessed the balding head to her left to be her father. Hank and Jenny were there, and Harry with a younger man who I guessed to be one of his sons.

Two women walked in, the younger one an echo of the older woman's top-heavy build and straight nose, but not her brassy blond hair. The mother was sobbing loudly and making a scene in the mostly quiet church. The young woman glanced around furtively as if looking for an escape.

"Jill Tiger Toes!" Gloria whispered.

"Jill?" I remembered the name from Anita's answering machine.

"Tiger Toes."

"You know her?"

"Spa client. She gets her toes painted with animal prints."

The service started and we were quiet. It was nice that they had a real pipe organ. The sound was much fuller than the electronic version, but I never understood why anyone would choose an organ over a piano.

The pastor had clearly never met Anita.

It was a relief when Jenny stood up to speak. She told a story about when Anita was six. She'd spent a rainy weekend with Jenny and Hank. Suited up in her yellow raincoat and rubber boots, she was splashing in puddles in the driveway when she discovered worms. She created a worm hospital in a shoe box, with beds of dirt and grass. She tended her patients carefully until the rain let up, then she found them homes in the garden. I wondered if Anita had been a born caregiver or whether she was modeling her own mother.

Hank spoke next. He told how Anita's childhood visits to Jaipur sparked her interest in gems. She also developed strong feelings about social class and felt passionately about the need for all people to have equal opportunities in life. She'd volunteered as a reading tutor in the Roxbury neighborhood of Boston, and like everything else, she did so quietly. She was a reserved, even shy, person, but that didn't mean she hid herself from life. She had excelled at single motherhood, career, and community, despite having lost her own mother at the age of sixteen.

"Why does history like to repeat itself?" I whispered to Gloria.

Anita certainly came off well. Most people seem to at their funerals. I hoped my friends would be skilled at rosy revisionism, because I couldn't even manage a committed relationship. I had a long way to go before motherhood and the halo.

When the service was over I caught Dani's eye as she walked up the center aisle. Her face was puffy and tear-stained. I felt my stomach clench, but the psychologist in my head said: *It's good that she's processing her grief. Crying is the best thing for her now.* I wished the psychologist would shut up. But this could be a big step for Dani. She might move toward accepting her mom's accident and let go of the denial phase of grieving that was pushing her to ask so many questions.

Standing in the pew waiting to file out of the church, I clasped my hands and sent up a prayer to the god managing this church. *Please move Dani to acceptance and help her find some peace in the truth.*

Brian passed us on his way out of the church. He was wearing his academic-safari wear. He looked pale and disheveled, as if he hadn't showered and changed for the service.

If the burial had been someplace else, we could have gotten out of it, but it was in the cemetery adjacent to the church. The ground was wet from storms the previous night, so women in heels wobbled and tottered and stuck. Jill Tiger Toes had an especially hard time, and when we passed her I got a big whiff of gin.

Gloria and I stood near the back of the crowd, but I could see Dani with her dad, Chris, who wasn't much taller than Dani and had a paunch of a stomach overhanging his black Dockers. He was stone-faced, and I couldn't imagine him younger, handsome, or smiling. What had the beautiful Anita seen in that guy? Next to him was a short, squarish woman dressed in pastel pink. She looked like one of those chalky after-dinner mints.

Dob and Josephine were front and

center, moving toward the two short rows of folding chairs set up under an awning. Dob hadn't seen me yet, and Josephine was glued to his side looking strained. Hank and Jenny stood to the side of the covered area, gauging the number of seats and waiting for others to take their seats first. An Indian-looking woman in a dark silk sari and a ginger-complected man with a matching tie and pocket square took seats under the awning.

Harry and his son were in the crowd to my left. Harry was teary, and his son looked bored. I caught Harry's eye and gave him a little smile.

Jill and her daughter had arrived behind us and stood to our right, closer to the awning. Jill teetered on the wet soil in her spiked heels and whispered too loudly, "God, let this be quick."

A man two people to my left spoke in a low voice to the person next to me. "She falls apart at funerals. Ever since J.J. died she seems to have to drink her way through." My heart softened a little. Who was I to judge people's behavior under stress? Just because I didn't like her dye job didn't mean she didn't have feelings and struggles. I promised myself I'd be more compassionate.

The graveside service was short. When the pastor had spoken everyone stood and the men began to lower the casket.

Then Josephine cracked. "God bless her heathen soul!" she screeched and turned to bury her face in her husband's chest, but he stepped back and she stumbled forward, tripped, and landed hands and knees in the piled-up dirt. There was a collective gasp. Dob hesitated a few beats, his face turning radish-red, then he leaned down and helped her up. She was sobbing, but whether it was from embarrassment or grief I couldn't tell. Dani watched the scene with big eyes. I thought about how everyone seemed to be all about themselves, and Dani was so alone. I wished I could at least stand by her, but I would have to wait to try and help her if she was able to come back to see me at work. That was a big "if."

Dob took Josephine's arm and began to walk her back toward the church—toward me. I tugged Gloria's elbow and backed away at an angle, hoping to hide in the crowd. I was too late. Dob caught sight of me and let out a low hiss. "You! I told you to stay away from this family. You have no right intruding on this service."

I continued my backward trajectory with Gloria following suit. Josephine, covered in dirt, said, "Dob, help me!" I had no doubt he'd rather berate me than help her, but he turned back to walk her to their car.

"Mother Mary!" Gloria said. "Dani is staying with that Hell Boar?"

"Do you think he's broken up about his sister?"

"Maybe that's Protestant grieving," she said, "but it looks like 'asshole' to me."

Harry approached us from behind. "Penny, so good to see you. It seems the family is not on their best behavior today, but then grief does bring out strange behavior, no?" He turned to his son and continued, "I want you to meet Thomas, my middle son." He turned to his son. "Thomas, this is Penny and..."

"This is my friend Gloria," I filled in. "Nice to meet you, Thomas." Thomas smiled with his mouth but not his eyes. In fact, his eyes looked too dull to smile. What a shame for lovely Harry to have such a dud of a son.

"We'd best be on our way, but I do hope you'll stop by the shop and see me again sometime. It was good of you to be here, I know Dani appreciates it. Oh, here she is now."

Dani was with the ginger man and Indian woman. She accepted a hug from Harry and introduced us all in a subdued voice. "These are Mom's cousins, Leena and Niles." Niles was smallish, and the prissy suit certainly didn't help his masculinity. Leena was beautifully rounded, with calm eyes and a motherly demeanor. She stood close to Dani and I could see a little family resemblance.

We gave our condolences and complimented the service. Harry asked, "Dani, do you need anything at all?"

She shook her head, keeping her eyes on the ground.

Niles said, "We'll take her back to Dob's and stay as long as she wants us there. Thanks for your kindness."

Everyone headed to the parking lot. Gloria and I brought up the rear.

"I guess we're not invited to the family gathering at Dob and Josephine's," Gloria said. "I was going to take her some lavender bath salts to calm the crazy."

We spent Sunday morning lounging around with coffee, arguing over old-fashioned cake donuts. It was nice to have Gloria around for once. She was a spa manager for a chichi place in the Back Bay and she kept very busy outside of work. Some people thought Gloria was flaky, but I thought she was resilient, if a little unfocused.

She was always dating someone, or multiple someones, and when things didn't work out she just moved on. In the worst case she might spend an evening weeping over a couple of beers and a bag of salt-and-vinegar chips, but the next morning she'd have that characteristic wag in her tail and she'd head out into the world to find out what came next.

"That was quite a party you took me to yesterday," she teased. "A bit short on attractive men though."

I laughed. "Let's not talk about it."

"Let's say someone did kill Anita. Just for the hell of it, let's play detective."

I was already thinking about it too much. I'd watched too many crime shows on TV.

"No, Gloria, she wasn't killed. I'm sick of trying to point that out."

Gloria ignored me. "Unless she was in a mood to let strangers into her house and eat what they offered, I'm guessing she knew the person."

I tapped excess powdered sugar off a doughnut into the box. "I don't want to talk about it."

We were both looking at Ranger, who

was pacing the hardwood floor between us and his food bowl. It was a waiting game to see who hauled herself up to feed him.

"Harry's son looked creepy. I wonder if he was the one who wants to take over the jewelry business."

I didn't respond.

Gloria got up and dumped some food into Ranger's bowl. I gave myself one small victory for the day, figuring it was all I would get.

"Tell me about Jill," I said. "She seemed overwrought."

Gloria plopped back down on the couch, looked into her mug, groaned, and got back up. "Being drunk didn't help her out. I heard her brother committed suicide a few years back. Can't be easy."

"That's terrible. Poor woman."

She looked at me over the kitchen island as she poured her coffee. "Well, miss bleeding heart, don't go overboard. Rumor has it she likes married men. Anyway, I don't know a whole lot about her, just snippets that I catch. She works for wealthy clients, that much is clear—maybe interior design or something."

I wondered if rumor was fair to Jill. I liked a married man once, but I didn't have an affair with him. I think the rumor mill had told a different story though.

"If Dani listens to Dob, I guess I won't hear from her."

"Why would she listen to Dob? Speaking of Dob, how about him and that freak of a wife?"

"Will you toss me a banana?" I asked. Gloria was sitting on a stool on the breakfast bar side of the island, probably to keep proximity to the coffee pot.

She tossed a banana and I caught it. Two victories in one day.

"Maybe Josephine was freaking out because her husband killed his own sister," she said.

"Stop, okay, Gloria?" I was starting to itch. I get hives under stress sometimes. "I have enough to worry about with Dani in denial, and stuck with Dob and Josephine."

After moping around the house all morning, eating too much sugar and getting uncomfortably wired on coffee, I pulled out my sluggish old laptop and checked email. I had a lot of offers to save on dresses, shoes, lamps, and office supplies. I unsubscribed from a couple and then got impatient and just started hitting delete.

Then I saw it. An email from Will. I stared at the screen. The subject said "Are you there?" I started to feel a bit under-oxygenated and realized I was holding my breath. It wasn't worth suffocating over. I clicked it open and read.

Penny. How are you? I'm fine. Still in Madison. Still cold. Jessica and I have been divorced for a year now. It's a good thing. What's new with you? I hope to hear from you.

Will was one of the few parts of my past I still found relevant. And remembered clearly.

I shut my computer and got up. The apartment was quiet; Gloria had gone in to work. I grabbed a towel from the hall closet and was headed to the bathroom when I heard a text message chime in on my cell phone.

There was just a phone number displayed, so it wasn't one of my contacts.

Can I c u? -Dani

I saved her number into contacts as I thought about how to respond. I texted back:

Me: Are you sure it's OK?

Dani: Yes. Bronze ducks@ 4?

Boston girl. I smiled. The statue commemorating the famous book *Make Way for Ducklings* was one of my favorite spots. It was always lively with children and there were several benches for top-notch people watching.

Me: OK.

I could probably have shortened it to "K," but I didn't find the "O" to be too much trouble.

I still had time for my bath and a little brooding over Will.

I arrived at the ducks right on time and lurked by a tree until a bench opened up. I snagged it and waited for Dani, feeling the chill of the cold metal bench seep through my jeans. She arrived in skinny jeans and a trim-fitting puffy jacket. Her hair was tucked up under a pink Red Sox cap. She smiled when she saw me, came over and sat.

"Thanks, Penny, I just really wanted someone to talk to. Harry said Mom's computer isn't at work and it's not at the apartment and I'm sort of freaked out."

"Did you go back there? Maybe you just didn't notice it when we were there."

Twin toddlers had arrived and were straddling two of the smaller ducks. Their dad was down on one knee trying to get them both in the picture without extraneous legs of passers-by.

"Dob took me over this morning to start packing stuff up. No computer, and I still couldn't find the family gems and stuff that my mom had hidden."

One of the twins decided that the other had a better duck, and was trying to push him off and gain ownership. Dani smiled a little at the scuffle.

"Did you talk to Hank?"

"Yep, I called him and told him. He said not to worry. He's gonna see what he can learn from the police tomorrow when the person he wants to talk to is back in the office. Why would someone steal her computer? I mean, I can see why someone would steal the gems and stuff…"

"Let's not get too far ahead. Maybe the police took the computer like Hank said they do in a normal investigation. And the gems are somewhere—a safe deposit box or something."

"But it wasn't an investigation! They wouldn't investigate!"

"We'll find everything."

The family with the twins had moved on, and some tweens were climbing on the ducks and joking loudly while parents of the younger kids glared and waited for them to move on too.

"Hey, I don't want you getting in trouble with Dob. Are you sure this is okay?"

"He and Josephine are at some country club benefit thingy all afternoon. They can't keep me captive."

"I know, but I'm just worried that you'll make matters worse for yourself since you have to stay there."

Dani just shrugged as if to say it would be okay, so I changed the subject. "Remember when Pack was stolen a few years ago?" Pack was the smallest bronze duck, the seventh in line.

"Yeah, they found him not far from Mom's shop on Mount Vernon Street." She paused. "I'm sort of worried about Harry. Mom said the shop has been having a really hard time since the recession. Now he doesn't have her and I think she was a really important part of the business."

"You'll stay in touch with him, won't you? I could tell you mean a lot to him."

"Yeah. Assuming I can stay here. My dad just can't make me go back to Philly! I don't want to go, and why would my mom leave Dob as the executor if she wanted my dad to take care of me?" She paused while we watched a dog chase a squirrel. It reached the end of its retractable leash with a jerk and fell back. Dani scrunched her face. "My dad and Dob had a big fight about the money last night after everyone had left the house. I could hear shouting from down the hall. My dad said she should have left him in charge since he was my father and would have custody of me. He said that Mom had tried to ruin his business, now this. I have no idea what he was talking about. Mom and Chris barely even spoke to each other—she didn't have anything to do with his business." She twisted her necklace as she spoke. "My dad has a bad temper. I can remember him yelling at my mom when I was a kid."

She stood up and said, "Can we walk a little?"

"Sure." I stood and we started walking toward the swan boat pond. It was drained for the winter and it never failed to amuse me to see that it was only a couple of feet deep.

"What would you do if you stayed here? Live with Dob and Josephine?"

"I can get a job or use some of my trust to get a little studio. I can take care of myself."

I knew that would never fly with her dad and Dob, and I didn't think she was as independent as she pretended.

We walked in silence for a little while. The Public Garden was one of my favorite places in the world. But as much as I hoped to stay in Boston forever, I would never be *of* Boston. In truth, I was a little intimidated by Boston natives because they had an inborn advantage I didn't. Kind of like people with good parents: they had an advantage so huge I'd never be able to make up for my relative lack. Two clubs to which I would never belong.

CHAPTER FIVE

Monday was a typical work day for me. Clients, paperwork, more clients, more paperwork. The highlight was grabbing a sandwich for lunch with Nathan, who was sporting a tiger sweatshirt. A tiger seemed like a nice strong start for a Monday. I brought him up to date on Dani. I asked him if I should tell Vivian what was happening and about Dob's threat to complain. He didn't preach to me about getting too involved, but he said maybe we should hold off on talking to Vivian. If Dob went to Vivian, Nathan would tell her that I'd reached out to him for help. I knew I could count on Nathan, but I was worried about Vivian, and Nathan's strategy for managing her confirmed that she wouldn't like what I was doing.

I'd planned to use the late afternoon for finishing paperwork, but Dani texted that she'd be by after school so I postponed it.

When she bobbed into my office I said, "Up for a walk?"

"Sure!"

She chattered while I got ready to go. "I saw my voice teacher today. He gave me some scores I can practice until I can take lessons again."

"Nice," I said. "Is that why you're all smiles? What are the songs?"

"'All I Ask of You' from *Phantom of the Opera,* and 'I've Never Been in Love Before' from *Guys and Dolls.*"

"I'm glad you can keep working," I said. "I'm sure you'll get your lessons back before too long."

The day was fading to a darker shade of the already gray gloom. We turned onto D Street and I noticed a man on the corner staring at Dani as we passed. People stared at Dani a lot; she had a slightly exotic look with her cat-tilted eyes and her gorgeous latte skin. So men staring wasn't unusual, but it made me nervous. Dani was obviously not well supervised in Dob and Josephine's care, and she was often alone around the city.

We walked down toward Moakley Park. The darkening sky was so low I could feel it like a dense wet wrap.

"How was dinner with your mom's cousins?"

"It was good. They're really nice. They come to the US a few times every year. They gave me some pictures of Mom that they took when she was in India. They said they wanted to show me my ancestral land someday. Isn't that funny? I have an ancestral land."

"It's very cool that you have family who not only love you, but are really interesting too."

"Niles grew up in London. He and Leena met in college. My mom told me about their big traditional Indian wedding. Mom and Leena were pretty close growing up so she got to be in the wedding. I think that was before I was born." She was rubbing her mittened hands together. "Yesterday Niles was telling me how a lot of the Indian food here isn't like in India. He said chicken tikka masala was actually invented in Great Britain. I love Indian food even if it isn't authentic. I hope I get to go there someday."

I glanced behind us for the third or fourth time. Someone turned a corner a block back, but I didn't see anything to justify the creepy feeling I had. Maybe it was just the dark day. Icy wind blew in off of Old Harbor. We walked a little faster to keep warm.

"I called Uncle Hank after school," she said. "The police don't have Mom's laptop. They said there was no evidence of a break-in. Their interview with Brian was short because they didn't suspect anything other than accidental death, but it said he had tried to revive her and that he wasn't very cooperative with the police. The rest of the stuff we already knew."

She lowered her voice and I had to lean in to hear her. "I have Mom's calendar for Uncle Hank, and her address book. He's coming in to town this evening to visit with Dob and Josephine and I'll sneak it to him somehow so he can see if there are any clues."

She turned and walked almost sideways and I could tell she was going to ask me for something. "I got Jill's number from my mom's book," she said. "I thought maybe since she was Mom's friend she might be able to tell us if anything was going on with her.

Since you're so good at asking questions, do you think you could come with me to meet her? I'll just tell her you're an old friend of Mom's who came in town for the funeral or something. Maybe she even saw you there."

We reached the park and crossed over to the water side of the street and sat on a bench facing into the biting wind. A small V of geese flew over and I marveled at their hardiness. Dani's cell bleeped and she read a text. "I've gotta get going. Josephine's home and wants to know where I am."

"I'll walk you to the T," I said, evading the question about Jill.

We got up and walked toward the Broadway station. "Please, Penny, I know I ask a lot, but I don't know how to do this alone and I'm afraid I'll just start crying. At least if you're there I don't have to talk as much. It's really hard for me to say… well, you know, to talk about her being gone with other people."

"Is this about murder?"

"No. I just want to see my mom's friend and see if I can understand what was happening before she died, okay?" She was dragging the toggles up and down the drawstring on her jacket hood.

I'd have to figure out how to put up a better guard—either that or just give in for good. "Okay, but don't get in any trouble. Does Jill know Dob?"

"Yeah, but I don't think she'd tell him and even so, why couldn't I see my mom's friend? I'll set it up after school, okay? Can you get away at four again one day?"

"I'll try, but I can't keep missing work, so if I have an appointment that I can't rearrange I won't be able to do it." I silently promised myself I would only go if my schedule was open.

"Got it," she said. "You don't have to walk me the rest of the way."

I watched her go, inspecting everyone on the street for potential danger. She finally turned a corner out of sight and I realized I couldn't stop the rush-hour stream of strangers who all seemed like threats.

I was left with my thoughts walking home through the cold streets. Will. I had no idea what outcome I was hoping for. I'd known him for ten years and I still got sappy fluttery feelings when I thought about him. But maybe it was because I couldn't have him—at least not back then. If we got back together I'd probably get sick of him in a couple of years, or he would get sick of me. I hadn't made the best choices about men thus far, and I didn't want to risk getting involved with another wrong guy. I wanted kids, but I didn't want to be like my parents: barely speaking to each other and fighting when they did. I remembered hearing their fights down the hallway from my bedroom. They would try to keep their voices low and I could never hear what they said, but I could sense their angry tones and I always thought they were fighting about me.

I thought about stories Nathan had told me about growing up in his tightly packed neighborhood in Detroit. The community was close and gossipy and kids couldn't get away with anything without a neighbor calling to tell their parents. "If you snuck out behind the garage and lit a cigarette," he told me once, "you'd hear the phone ring in the kitchen." I smiled at the memory of his story. I wouldn't have liked that as a kid, but at least I would have known somebody cared about what I was doing.

I wished there were nosy neighbors watching out for Dani.

When I got home I made a cup of tea and opened my computer. My stomach quavered a little as I hit "reply" to Will's note and wrote:

Hey Will, glad all is well with you. Things are fine here. I left Juvie for a social work job and it's keeping me really busy. So you and Jessica divorced, huh? You never mentioned...

Well, I didn't just write it. I wrote it and revised it four times and that's where I landed. I thought it was friendly but not too friendly and sort of left an opening without asking him to write back.

I checked email when I woke up Tuesday morning. Nothing from Will. I shouldn't have checked because not having email from someone who really isn't your love interest anyway (because it really is ancient history) is a crappy way to start the day.

At lunchtime I retrieved a text from Dani.

Dani: 4:30 thinking cup on common.
Me: K

Getting hipper all the time.

I was late getting to the coffee shop

because I couldn't get out of the office. Dani and Jill were sitting at a four-top against the front window when I arrived. Jill was leaning across the table looking at Dani with such affection that I wondered how close she had been to Anita and Dani. I stopped at the counter and ordered organic green tea to keep the jitters down. I was on the lookout for whatever information might settle Dani's mind. Maybe Jill would help.

Jill held out her hand and introduced herself. Her armful of bracelets jangled as we shook hands. I remembered that I was supposed to be a friend from out of town but I'd forgotten to think up a story. I remembered that Anita had gone to Lesley—maybe I knew her there before I moved away to become a famous fashion designer in New York. Well, a little famous. Jill's voice broke through my mental scramble. "…at Lesley so many years back. We've been dear friends ever since." Oh geez, I guess I didn't go to Lesley.

"I'm so glad to finally meet you," I said, trying to buy time. "I've heard such nice things from Anita. I'm a friend of her family friends, the Dorians, at least that's how Anita and I met, and we just sort of kept up over the years. I haven't seen her for a couple of Christmases. I can't believe we won't see her again." I tried not to lay it on too thick because I was afraid I'd upset Dani and screw up any hope at regaining equilibrium.

"Anita spoke of you too," she lied politely. "Remind me, where do you live?"

"Oh, I'm in a sleepy suburb outside of

Indianapolis now. Carmel." At least by naming my home town I had a place I knew something about.

I turned and looked at Dani and smiled hello. "So, I guess you've known Dani since she was born too, huh?"

"I have. She was a tiny thing with those huge dark eyes and improbably long eyelashes. She was quite a star. Everyone adored her—everyone still does."

"I remember how she used to boogie like a disco star when she was about three." I considered it improv, not lying. I had to play along, after all.

"She always loved music," Jill said.

"Okay, you can stop talking about me like I'm not here," Dani said.

Jill laughed. "Okay, Dani. It's just so good to see you. Is there anything I can do to help you? The service was lovely, by the way, as hard as I know it was for you." She looked sincerely concerned for Dani and I felt a stab of guilt for lying to her. She had more right to be Dani's friend than I did.

"Did you know Anita's allergy was life-threatening?" I asked. "I guess I didn't realize —"

"I knew it was serious," she said. "I was always nervous in restaurants with her."

I tried to think about how to keep us focused on the accident so Dani could hear how Jill and I accepted the cause of death and realize she should too. But Dani jumped in before I could keep control of the conversation.

"I just wanted to talk with you because

I noticed that for a couple of weeks before Mom died she was really nervous and stuff. So I asked you two for coffee since you were both her friends, and I thought you might know what was going on with her."

Jill clasped her hands together on the table. She rubbed at one thumbnail with the other thumb. "Oh, Dani, I'm sure it was nothing. Things just get stressful as an adult sometimes, you know? When you have responsibilities and you don't know if you're doing a good job—money gets tight or you're worried about people you love. If it had been more than normal stress she would have mentioned it to me."

Dani persisted. "I know what Mom was like when she was stressed over money or how I was doing in school. This was different. Worse."

"Well," Jill said, "you know, there was one thing she mentioned." She touched her forehead and reclasped her hands. "She and Brian had been quarreling. Did you know he had proposed?"

Dani shook her head and so did I.

"She turned him down and he was pretty upset. I thought she was too good for him anyway, but she didn't want to break up, she just didn't want to get married. She was probably protecting her inheritance and your future, Dani. She was careful about that. She loved you so very much."

I didn't like what might be going on in Dani's head. "Did you know Brian well?" I asked. "I only met him briefly. He seemed like a nice guy."

"Oh, well enough. He's a bit of a know-it-all, but most academics are. I'm just not sure how stable he is. He lost his wife several years back and maybe he never recovered."

Poor Dani was wide-eyed and silent. I was glad I was there with her. "I have to say I wasn't in close enough contact with your mom to know what was going on recently, Dani," I bluffed, "but remember, couples have these kinds of disagreements all the time. Even though she said no, she loved him and was probably happy he'd asked. Don't you think, Jill?"

Jill was fidgeting with her cup. She shrugged and said, "She might have been flattered he asked. By the way, I saw Niles and Leena at the service. It was nice of them to come all this way."

"Yeah, I like having them here. Leena's my closest family on Mom's side now. She's really sad."

Jill checked her blingy watch and said, "I should be getting back. I'm sorry to make this so short, but you have my number, Dani. Please call any time if I can do anything for you, and I'd love to have coffee more often."

"It was nice of you to get away," I said. "It was great to meet you. Do you work nearby?"

"Oh, I work here and there, and I like to haunt the Back Bay boutiques when I can." She smiled.

We said goodbyes and Dani and I stayed to finish our drinks. "What does Jill do for a living?" I asked.

"She's a stylist."

I raised my eyebrows.

"She helps really rich people with their clothes and jewelry and even their homes and parties, I think."

I thought about that for a minute. Dani watched me and broke into a smile. "I know, she looks a little trashy, but Mom said she does a really good job for people. Not like her personal style. Jill's pretty nice."

Boston foot traffic was at its evening height as Dani and I dodged along the sidewalk. I could smell the ocean air coming off the bay. I understood why Dani never wanted to leave. In Boston you could work a crossword in a pub with a guy from Southie and sit on a park bench with an Iranian MIT professor discussing the concert series at the Hatch Shell in the same afternoon.

Where I grew up there were the "right people" to socialize with and it was clear who they were. The problem for me was that I was expected to circulate among the "desirables," but I never liked them. I envied the way Dani had been comfortably raised among this diversity.

"Jenny and Hank invited me and you to dinner tomorrow night," she said when we got out of the foot traffic enough to walk side by side. "Can you go with me? Can you take me?"

I hesitated, but I was beginning to see that I was going to help Dani for as long as I could. "Sure, as long as it isn't too early."

"They said six thirty, okay?"

"We'll leave here at five thirty along with all the commuters. That should give us time."

When I got home Gloria was in the kitchen and I smelled curry. Heaven. "Hey, Gloria," I said, dropping my bag inside the door. "It smells great in here."

"I wondered if you were coming," she said. "I made red curry with tofu and veggies. The rice is almost done, then we'll be ready to eat."

"Thanks, wow. This is great." I let out a big breath and sank onto the couch.

"Everything okay?"

"Not sure."

"Something food can cure?"

"What can't food cure?" I could hope.

Gloria smiled and read my mind. She poured me a glass of wine and brought it to me. "Well, some stuff, but wine might fill in where food leaves off."

"Dangerous attitude," I said, accepting the glass and taking a sip.

"If all else fails we'll pull out the big guns: aromatherapy."

We sat down to dinner. I didn't want to talk about Dani or murder or work. Gloria's curry was delicious, the carrots were tender but not mushy, the potatoes had absorbed the red curry flavors, and the tofu was firm enough to give the dish some weight. Still, I found myself picking at it. "Will emailed," I said before my internal censor could stop me.

"Oh? What did he say?"

"He's divorced. They divorced over a year ago."

"*Dios mio*, that *is* news. And he's letting you know now. Maybe your planets are syncing back up."

I didn't really know what that meant, but I let it go because I didn't want an astrology lesson. "I guess. I don't know what to think. It would be stupid to entertain anything with him still in Madison."

"Couples have overcome worse." Gloria had finished half her plate and I was still picking.

"Yeah, but we're not a couple and I'm not a great overcomer when it comes to relationships."

My phone interrupted us. I didn't recognize the number.

"Hello?"

"Penny, this is Dob Nayak. Is Dani with you?"

My breath caught in my throat. It had been almost two hours since we boarded the T. She should have been home a long time ago.

"No, she's not."

He must have heard the worry in my voice and believed me because he didn't challenge me. He just hung up.

I texted Dani:

Me: You okay? Dob is worried

I cranked up the phone volume so I wouldn't miss if she texted back.

I explained to Gloria as I paced the floor. I put on my jacket and took it off. Where would I even look? I didn't have phone numbers for any of her friends. I didn't know where they hung out. Maybe I should hit the coffee shops near her school?

"She's sixteen," Gloria said. "She's like

smoking cigarettes with a friend or something. Don't worry."

I decided to believe Gloria. I pulled out my Tyrannosaurus laptop to distract myself. Will had emailed.

Hi Penny, I hope you had a good Tuesday. I met with some difficult clients, then sacrificed half the good elements in the design for their copy. All in a day's work. I have been finding a little time for my own art, a remedy to being a slave to the man. I've already started planning the garden—a little early, I know. Tell me about you. – W.

I thought about him grumbling over his computer, running his fingers absently through his chestnut curls leaving them even wilder than before. Graphic design is not heaven for creatives, it turns out. Will always struggled, but he was good with clients and great at his job, so he stayed. Madison was one of those places where people go to college, then stay for another degree, then stay some more. It rivaled Boston in over-education, so finding a good job there was especially hard. Will loved the lakes and the ability to live in a quiet rural location, but still be close to town. I wondered if it would feel safer to raise kids in a rural place—if we were in a tiny town I'd probably know where to look for Dani.

"Well?" Gloria broke into my daydreaming. "Note from Will?"

"Yeah, just about his day." I read her the note.

"Hmmm. Are you going to write right back?"

"May as well, this came in this

morning."

"Don't be cold, Penny, okay? He's gorgeous and smart and single. Tauruses are loyal to the bone. He's a man you could have some serious stability with. At least play along a little and see how you feel." Gloria had met Will when he visited Boston a few times over the years. She'd always thought I should pursue him.

"I won't be cold." The trouble was I already knew how I felt—fluttery and distracted and ultimately confused. So I guessed the confused part was the part I was waiting out.

I started to write back, but I couldn't concentrate because I couldn't shake my anxiety about Dani. I called her. No answer.

Then I rewrote my email to Will: *I envy your garden planning. The wait list for a plot in the Victory Gardens is long, and when would I get over there to tend it? It is one of my favorite places though. I'll have to settle for strolling through, looking at other people's gardens. My Tuesday was strange. New job is heavy. –Penny*

It was surprisingly easy to fall back into the old rhythm with him. For years before our recent silence we'd stayed in almost daily contact, sharing little things—sick with a cold, the rain won't stop, made vegetable lasagna, the lady at the DMV made me cry, and so on. We'd been friends through our respective other relationships, and sometimes, even when I was in a relationship, it seemed like Will knew more about my life than my boyfriend did. Still, we weren't back in the groove enough for me to trouble him with my worries about Dani.

I turned on the TV and flipped through channels, trying to get my mind off of images of Dani in the clutches of a killer. The only thing I could find that didn't give me even more scary thoughts was a home renovation show, but it couldn't hold my attention. I thought about all the things that could go wrong: someone snatched her on the T; she met up with friends and got drunk and in trouble; she got fed up with Dob and Jo and ran away. What if she caught a train to New York? There were so many dangers I couldn't imagine and didn't want to.

Gloria watched me fidgeting, channel flipping, and repeatedly checking the fridge. When she couldn't take it anymore she sat down to give me a wise-friend talk.

"You know, it was only two generations ago when my abuela and other women were raising children and running households and farms at sixteen."

"I think there were fewer threats on the farm," I interrupted.

"No. There were plenty of dangers. When my mom was a baby, Abuela had her on her back while she worked in the field. She was bitten by a snake. Nobody was around and she couldn't walk. She had to drag herself back to the house with Mom on her back crying. She had to treat the wound herself while she waited for my abuelo to get home."

Worry coursed through me like chemical heat. There were more snakes on the Boston T than in a Mexican farm field.

Finally a text rang in.

Dani: I'm fine. Home now.

"I almost forgot to tell you," Gloria said from the kitchen. "I overheard some ladies dishing at the spa today. Josephine Nayak is having an affair—with a very young man, no less."

CHAPTER SIX

        The Zipcar selection was slim Wednesday evening. Dani and I ended up in a blue Ford Focus. My shoulders were incredibly tense and I was cursing at the traffic getting out of town. When we finally got on I-90 I asked her, "Where were you last night?" I glanced over and her eyes were on the road.
        "I was just at a friend's."
        "Why didn't you tell someone? Why didn't you tell me? I texted. Why didn't you answer?"
        "I forgot to turn my phone on after school, okay?"
        I remembered being interrogated like that at her age, but the words kept coming and I was upsetting myself even more by sounding like my mom.
        "I was worried," I said.
        "I'm *sorry*, I was just at a friend's house. I can take care of myself!"
        I was upset about arguing with Dani, but I relaxed a little when we walked into Hank and Jenny's home and smelled wood fire and sage. Hank greeted us with hugs and hurried back to the kitchen. Jenny poured a soda for Dani and a glass of red wine for me and we sat in big overstuffed chairs in the

living room looking out huge windows at their woodsy yard lit by floodlights. "Leena and Niles are coming," Jenny said, "I can't remember if I told you that."

Dani said, "That's great!" and smiled a sparkly smile.

I eyed the baby grand at the end of the long room. "Who plays piano?"

"Hank plays brilliantly and I try," Jenny replied. "It keeps me humble. Do you play?"

"No. I never learned."

"It's never too late. I've learned many things late in life, and you're still young."

The doorbell rang and Jenny went to answer. She returned with Niles and Leena. Dani exchanged hugs with both and I was reintroduced. Leena took Dani's hand and the two sat together on the couch. Niles sat in an armchair by the fire. He was proper and petite in the huge chair, but not stiff. He beamed at Dani. I got the impression that he and Leena had known Hank and Jenny for a long time.

Hank came in with a tray of cheese and crackers. He'd already spread the soft cheese on some of the crackers and he passed the tray before setting it on the coffee table and settling into one of the big chairs. His smile was indulgent, but his eyes didn't match it. I could tell he wanted to tell us something. I took a deep breath and concentrated on the creamy brie before things got serious.

"I know it may not be the best manners, but I don't want to keep you waiting on what I've learned since we spoke last." He glanced at Jenny, who didn't seem to disapprove. He turned to Niles and Leena and added, "Dani has some questions about Anita's death. I've done a little checking so that we can clear things up." He turned back to Dani. "You already know Boston PD didn't confiscate Anita's computer. They also confirmed that there was no EpiPen present. They probably should have treated it like a crime scene just in case, but they didn't. I'm not saying it was a crime scene, just that they should have been more thorough."

"She always had EpiPens," Leena said.

Hank paused. Dani was at that age where it didn't make sense to protect her like a child, but there was still reason for caution.

I had to jump in. "But it was clear that it was an accident and—"

Dani interrupted me. "Uncle Hank, did you look at Mom's calendar?"

"I did, and nothing jumps out at me, but it's always hard to tell what will become useful. Thank you for your stealth drop. I'm sorry we had to be evasive about that, but I don't want Dob and Josephine to worry unnecessarily."

"That's thoughtful of you," Niles said. "They're under so much stress already."

"Penny and I had coffee with Mom's friend Jill yesterday," Dani said. "She said that Mom and Brian had been fighting a lot because Brian wanted to get married and Mom didn't. She seems like she doesn't really like Brian."

"Have you seen Brian?" Hank asked. "Or talked to him?"

"Penny and I saw him at the apartment. He was picking up his stuff at the same time I was. He didn't have her laptop with his stuff. He told me about finding her too late, and there was no EpiPen. He was at the funeral too, but I only saw him from a distance. Maybe he didn't want to talk because I was with my dad?"

I couldn't tell, but I thought she seemed a little hurt. I was still trying to get a bead on how she felt about Brian.

"Did you see him there?" Dani asked Hank.

"We did see him and extended condolences, but that was really all we had time to do," he said. "I think he left after the church service. He looked like he was taking it really hard. Maybe we can reach out to him. What do you think, Jenny?"

"Sure," Jenny answered. "We know him well enough to extend an invitation for lunch and see how he's doing. Dani, do you think he could have the computer at his place? Maybe Anita had been over there?"

"Maybe." Dani's voice was soft and hesitant. "But I don't know why she would. She always stayed at home—he came to our house." She leaned forward for a cracker and regarded it with too much interest. "Do you know how Brian's wife died? I never heard him talk about it."

Leena answered. "My understanding is she died of breast cancer. She was quite young, in her thirties."

"We didn't know Brian well," Niles added, "but Anita spoke very highly of him. They seemed well matched in many ways."

We were all quiet for a moment. It had

gotten fully dark out since we'd been sitting there and the fire was reflected in the big window. I could smell bread baking and my stomach started to growl.

Hank rose and put another log on the fire and invited us into the dining room.

The centerpiece of the room was a long pine farm table that would seat twelve or more. But next to the window was a more intimate table, set with flowers, rich red napkins, and warm brown earthenware plates. "We sit here most of the time," Jenny said, "but the farm table is wonderful for big gatherings. We used to host Thanksgiving dinner every year when Dani was a little girl. We've shared a lot of holidays with your family here, haven't we, Dani?"

"I remember sitting on my grandpa's lap at that table," Dani replied, "and you and Mom were always in the kitchen." She turned to me. "Sometimes Leena and Niles were here too!" She smiled at Leena, who nodded and looked like she was blinking back tears.

Now Dani's grandpa and mother were both gone. The loss hung heavy in the room.

"That was before I taught Hank to cook." Jenny's smile broke the tension. "I should have done it sooner!"

"Your grandpa was my favorite uncle," Leena said. "He always played with us, even when the other adults were too busy with each other."

Hank came in with a pasta dish made with butternut squash and sage; salad; and fresh rolls. He refilled drinks and sat.

"Dani, I assume you got to spend some

time with your dad. How was that?"

"It was okay, I guess. He kept asking if Brian was trying to contact me. I guess my dad didn't like Brian either. He wants to take me to live with him and Linda in Philly as soon as school gets out for winter break. I don't want to go. But I really hate living with Dob and Josephine." She paused and rolled her napkin ring across her placemat. "I wish my mom had left me a guardian. I wish she'd left me to you."

The words stopped spilling and Dani looked a little sheepish, as if she hadn't meant to say that last part, but Jenny jumped right in.

"I do too, Dani, I really do." Jenny was teary and Hank had the concerned helpless look that men get when there's too much emotion in the room. Niles was studying his plate, and Leena watched Dani.

I wondered if Dani felt safe with Dob and Josephine. If Josephine was having an affair there was potential for a lot of trouble in that house.

After dinner we returned to the living room and Dani asked Leena how often Anita used to go to India as a kid.

"Anita and Dob would spend six weeks or so with us every summer," Leena said. "We weren't allowed to play out in the streets like other kids because we were kept under tight security. We had a few cousins and family friends who would come to our home and play, but it was always nice to have more kids and Anita was my favorite cousin."

"You had to stay home?" Dani asked.

"Did you have a big yard?"

"We had some grounds around our house, and it was all walled in. The guards would let us play out there. My favorite outside game was called 'Chain.' Whoever was 'it' ran and caught someone and then the two ran holding hands to catch the hand of the next person and so on. The last person who got caught won. When Anita and Dob were there our chain would get to eight or nine children. It was fun to try to run like that."

"My mom taught me a clapping game," Dani said.

"Probably Chehmma Checka," Leena replied. "Do you remember it?"

Leena moved to where Dani was sitting, kneeled facing her, and went through the hand motions in the air. Dani joined her and the two clapped the rhythm together until they dissolved into giggles.

I could easily imagine Leena as a little girl and I wondered what it was like for her to relive the game with Anita's likeness.

"We used to play games like this in the courtyard," she said, "and when it was really hot we'd lie on the cool tile floor of the veranda and eat pomegranates and play Uffangali."

"What's that?" Dani asked.

"It translates like 'blow seeds.' You make a pile of tamarind seeds in the middle and each person takes a turn blowing as hard as they can—just one blow. You get to keep however many seeds you blow free of the pile. Whoever has the biggest pile when all the seeds are gone from the middle wins."

"So the only way to win is to blow the hardest?" Dani asked.

"The angle can make a difference too," Leena said.

As we were leaving I handed my card to Hank. When Dani turned to hug Jenny I gave him a raised eyebrow and looked at the card in his hand. He nodded, said goodnight, and we thanked them and left.

Hank called Thursday morning before my first client was scheduled. His voice sounded like he hadn't used it much yet. "Penny, Hank Dorian. I hope everything is okay."

"Thanks for calling. There's just something I wanted to talk about without worrying Dani." I grabbed a snowman snow globe off my table and shook it. "Dob visited me at my office on Friday. He told me in a rather intimidating manner that he wanted me to back off of my relationship with Dani."

"Oh?"

"He said I was encouraging her imagination. I assured him that my only goal is to help her process her mother's death in a healthy manner, but he insisted I stop seeing her and threatened to call my boss if I don't."

"And you haven't."

"No. Dani needs someone on her side and she asks for my help. I want to help her and I'm worried because she is uncomfortable at the Nayaks' house and Dob doesn't want her to continue her counseling."

I waited for him to speak.

"I don't know what to say, Penny. Dob is

taking care of her for now, and I'm sure he's just trying to protect her as best he knows how. I've known Dob all his life—he may get intense sometimes, but he's grieving the loss of his sister. He's not a threat. Perhaps you're overreacting?"

"Dob doesn't want Dani looking into how her mom died. I don't like the talk of murder, but Dani needs to have her questions answered. She won't be able to work toward acceptance if she continues to believe someone killed her mom."

"I'm helping her with the unanswered questions. I'm in a better position to do that. Perhaps you should lay low." His tone belied his diplomatic words. He was siding with Dob.

After we hung up I found myself standing by the window looking out at the nasty December sleet.

After work I headed to Beacon Hill to meet Toryn at Figs for dinner. He'd called the night before, and I realized that I was the one who was upset, not him. He was good old Toryn, happy to give me room to throw a fit and still be my friend. I got to the Hill early because I wanted to drop in on Harry at the jewelers'. The wind chime announced me and Harry looked up from a table behind the counter. He lowered a loupe from his eye and smiled.

"Penny, so good to see you. Will you have a seat? Some tea? I have the kettle on."

"Nice to see you too, and yes, I'd love a cup. I'm meeting a friend at Figs in a bit, so I took the excuse to come visit."

I heard a man's voice and looked

toward the back of the shop.

"That's Thomas on the phone in back," Harry said. "He's been working here more to fill in since we lost Anita. He has some ideas about how to do things a bit differently and he's been working hard."

"That must be nice. I'm glad you have someone to help out." I sat in one of the red chairs and Harry brought tea. He sat across from me. Thomas's voice rose in the back room, and Harry turned his head in that direction before returning his attention to me. He straightened the crease in his slacks and smiled politely.

"Tell me how our Dani is holding up. I wish I could do something to help the poor child."

"She's hanging in, but staying at Dob's wouldn't be her first choice. The problem is that she doesn't want to go live with her dad either." I shifted around to get comfortable in the big chair.

"Chris is a bit of a sod, I'm afraid. It's a bad situation indeed. There's reason to question Anita's choices in men. The only one I ever liked was a fellow named Josh. But that ended in disaster." He blinked hard and took a sip of tea. "Speaking of Anita and men, I had a call from Brian yesterday. It was odd, I'll say. I haven't entirely figured it out."

"Why did he call?"

"Well, that's not clear. At first it seemed simply social—he asked if I'd seen Dani, and how things were going at the shop without Anita. But then he told me that he had saved some research data on her laptop when he was doing work at her apartment and he needed to get it from her computer when he comes back in town—I think that was today he said he was coming back. I told him that her laptop wasn't here but he asked me to check again because he had checked the apartment. I hadn't thought about the fact that he would have a key, but of course, and I guess there's no harm in it."

"They'd been dating for something like two years, right?"

"Yes, something like that. I told him I had double checked and the computer isn't here. Then he asked a few sort of vague questions about how the shop is doing and if everything is okay. He was talking fast but not making a lot of sense to me. Anita's death has taken quite a toll on a number of people, I suppose. We revolved around her more than we realized."

"I wish I'd known her."

A customer came into the shop and Harry stood to greet her.

"I'll be on my way," I said. "It was great to see you. Take care."

"Thank you for coming by, Penny. Give Dani my love and come back soon."

I hit the sleety streets and found Toryn waiting outside of Figs with his jacket pulled up over his face, jumping up and down to stay warm.

"How long's the wait?" I asked.
"Forty-five."
"Crap. How long have you been here?"
"Six."
"Crap."

"What to do?"

"Sevens?"

"Sevens."

We crossed Charles Street and headed uphill to the Sevens, a traditional friendly Boston pub. Once inside, it took our eyes a moment to adjust. The pub was long and narrow, full of dark wood. The only windows were on the street front. It smelled of beer, cleaner, and fried food. Customers' heads were turned up to the Patriots game showing on several screens. We sat at the bar and ordered two Sam Adamses. Toryn crossed his long skinny legs and downed half of his beer, then asked what was new.

"Well, in newest news, I just came from visiting Anita's old boss, Harry. He said Brian called. For one thing, he was looking for Anita's computer. I guess that answers the question of whether he has it. I don't know what to make of any of it, but backing up, there are more and more suspicious circumstances and Dani is certainly not settled about how her mom died." I looked at my glass and noted that my beer was disappearing fast too.

"Well, that's one reason I wanted to get together. Yesterday I had coffee with the contact that helped me out with Anita's file. He told me that the file has been reopened. Someone high up the food chain made the request."

"Huh. A friend of Dani and Anita's family —Hank Dorian, she calls him Uncle Hank—is an ex–police chief from Wayland. He called BPD to get details on the case and see if they'd confiscated Anita's laptop. Maybe he encouraged them to take a second look. Unfortunately, I've gotten myself on his bad side and I'm not sure if I'm even going to see Dani because her real uncle has forbidden her to see me." Words were coming out fast, aided by the beer and the relief of having a good friend to confide in.

"So you're still pretty involved in this, huh?"

"I was, up until today. I really want to help her, Tor, she's living with her dastardly uncle, her dad says she has to go to Philly to live with him and his weird wife after winter semester, and the poor girl thinks someone killed her mom."

"I did learn one other thing from my friend," he said. "Anita's boyfriend was investigated after the death of his wife."

"I thought she died of cancer."

"Not exactly. She died of morphine overdose, as she was dying of cancer."

"Oh. That's… not good." My skin prickled and I could feel the threat of hives starting on my chest. "What happened with the investigation?"

"They were never able to pin it on him. There were multiple people administering her medication, and there was no strong evidence pointing to him." Toryn's eyes were glued to me. He usually took pleasure out of gossip, but not this time.

"Even if he did do it, though, it sounds like it could have been out of compassion, right?" I said. "Not like murdering Anita. Why would he murder Anita?"

"Why does anyone murder? Jealousy? Rage? Money? She knew a secret? He killed once and liked feeling like God? Who knows."

On Friday I hoped for a text from Dani, but I didn't hear a peep. I wanted to text her but worried that Dob may be checking her phone. It was a quiet day at work and I managed to clean up a lot of paperwork, then moved on to triage email. There was a note from Will.

Hey Penny, almost the weekend! Do you have plans? Anyone special in your life these days? I plan to work on a building project—redoing my laundry area—and try my hand at cooking risotto. Not terribly exciting, but enough, along with a couple of good books, to keep me busy. Hope to hear from you. –W.

I imagined Will standing at his stove reading while stirring. He would have a hard time mustering the patience for risotto unless he had a book. He kept at least one fiction and one nonfiction going at all times. He was always learning about something new, whether it was the consequences of factory farming, how underwater tunnels were constructed, or flora of Wisconsin. I remembered the two of us shoving piles of books off the bed in a moment of passion. That was one of my favorite memories with him. Will wasn't typically spontaneous—he was more the kind of guy that would ask before kissing a woman, to proceed respectfully. That appealed to my feminist sensibilities, but my feminist sensibilities didn't apply in the bedroom.

I shook myself from my reverie. No point in getting into that emotional space again. I didn't believe we could make something work, but at the same time I enjoyed falling back into the groove of being in touch with him. I emailed back.

No real weekend plans. I hope to sleep a lot. I hope Gloria cooks. I will have to tell you about what's been going on at work one of these days. I'm really tired. The answer to your other question is no. What are you reading? –P.

Early that afternoon I finally found Vivian free in her office. I had to tell her that Dob had called Lynnie and canceled Dani's appointments moving forward. I told her I was concerned about Dani's access to counseling. I tried to stay dispassionate so she wouldn't know how far I'd gotten involved.

Vivian addressed the problem with businesslike efficiency. She suggested we call Family Services to let them know. I was relieved that we could do something besides sit on our hands and wish things were different. Vivian picked up the phone and placed the call while I waited. DCF said that they would send someone to the Nayaks' to check in and make sure Dani was doing well, and to let the Nayaks know that they recommended short-term counseling for at least another few months.

"Now you can focus on the rest of your caseload, Penny," she said crisply. "The volume isn't getting any lighter around here."

I'd probably lose my job if she

discovered me ducking out early and calling in sick to help Dani. The rent wouldn't wait for me to find another job, and I was already reduced to ramen noodles at the end of each paycheck.

As I left her office Vivian said, "Penny, it can be dangerous to get too involved with clients. Your job is to do what you can when they're in session with you, and that's all."

I slumped back to my office, feeling ashamed about getting too involved but simultaneously indignant because without being involved I couldn't help.

The rest of the afternoon went by so slowly I thought my office clock's battery was dying. I thought about going to see Harry, but didn't know what good it would do. Then I had an idea. If Brian was back in town he was probably at work. I would go on a little errand to UMass. The only problem was that I should probably get there during the work day. I decided to be sick. I did have cramps a little, and I hadn't slept well worrying about Dani, so that could be considered sick.

I called up front to Lynnie to let her know I needed to cancel my last appointment and leave because I wasn't feeling well. I gathered my stuff and buzzed past her at the desk while she was on the phone.

I was shaping up to be a lousy social worker. It wasn't that I didn't care about my clients, only that most of them didn't care about therapy and didn't try at all. I'd gotten into this lousy-pay profession to help people and I was determined to do it. The clients who came in and lied to me and themselves were part of the deal, but I wasn't going to let them stop me from making a difference where I could.

Fortified and justified by my rationalizations, I headed to UMass. There was a little break in the cold and I felt energized by taking action. People were out walking dogs and jogging in the rare bit of sunshine. I found myself smiling in camaraderie with Bostonians.

The campus was built on a landfill peninsula jutting out into Old Harbor. The view of the city was great when you got a glimpse around the massive red brick buildings. The campus wasn't particularly attractive, but it was functional and a university education there was practically free to Massachusetts residents. I found the building with the History Department and checked the directory. I didn't know his last name so I was glad to see first names were listed. I hit the elevator button to the third floor.

Brian answered his office door quickly at my knock. He was in his uniform of tweedy sports coat atop tan cargo pants. He opened his mouth to say something before he looked up. He glanced up at me and stopped. I could see past him into the small office with its little square window. I smelled stale coffee and sweat.

"What the hell?"

At least he recognized me. "Were you expecting someone else? I'm hoping you have just a minute." I tried to step forward into the doorway but he blocked me squarely.

"I don't have a minute."

"Please," I said firmly, "I'm here for Dani."

He hesitated then stepped back, allowing me entrance into the glorified closet. He plopped into his worn desk chair and I sat in the only other chair, the one students must sit in when they came for help. If they came for help. I scratched at the hives on my neck.

"Dani is struggling," I said. "She can't accept her mom's death until she has a better understanding of what happened. Did you see anything that might help her to understand? Or do you know why Anita didn't have an EpiPen around? Dani said she always had EpiPens." I thought I sounded pretty calm given that I might be in a room with a murderer.

"And why are you asking me?" His jaw jutted forward, pushing out his lip in a gesture that was somehow childish and intimidating at the same time.

"Because you were close to Anita and you were the first on the scene. You've surely been trying to sort this out yourself."

He pivoted his desk chair toward the window, which was too high to see out when sitting and added to the prison cell effect of the office.

He turned back, frowning. "Look, miss, I want to be clear. The police were right. Like you said, I was the first on the scene and she had died of anaphylaxis. I see how it could be very hard for Dani to accept this and of course she wants an explanation but there isn't one. It was just a tragedy with no meaning, no explanation. She's got to stop asking questions and accept—"

There was a hard knock at the half-open door. I turned to see Dob filling the doorframe. His eyes widened when he saw me and his face flushed. I stood.

"Ms. Wade." His voice wasn't loud, but it had a thunderous quality no less. "May I have a word?" He gestured his head toward the hallway. I nodded and glanced at Brian. His eyebrows were knit and he pushed his glasses up his nose.

I stepped into the hallway in the shadow of the tower-of-Dob. Brian followed and leaned against the doorframe watching us. "You are, again, where you don't belong," Dob hissed in a near whisper. He was blinking a lot and his face had a sheen of sweat. He stooped to get even closer to me. Something in his eyes changed and suddenly it was as if he wasn't just threatening but also pleading. "Stay out of this." He swallowed hard. "Please."

I went to UMass to get information and if I couldn't get it from Brian maybe I could learn something from Dob.

"Why are you so set against me helping Dani through her mother's death?" I asked. "That's my job and she wants my help. Where's the harm?"

His face was impassive. "If you stayed in your office and provided normal counseling services that would have been fine." He shifted his weight and cleared his throat before continuing. "But now Dani is putting herself in danger on a crazy chase to find a murderer and you're complicit!"

I wasn't getting any info. "Do you believe Anita was murdered?" A little voice in the back of my head pointed out that asking a potential murderer that question with another potential murderer standing right there, no less, wasn't wise. I ignored it.

His ears reddened. "You have been watching too many crime shows on TV."

I opened my mouth before my next question had formed but he cut me off before I started.

"I didn't come here to talk to you. I have business to attend to." He turned to Brian and the two men stepped into the office and closed the door.

The JFK UMass T station is always busy and inbound trains come from two directions, merging just before the station. Instead of waiting on the platform, you wait in the lobby until a bell rings and an arrow tells you which platform to go to for the next train. When it's especially busy, as it was that evening, a whole crowd goes barreling down the steps to compete for spots on the packed train. If you aren't aggressive sometimes you don't make it and have to go back up the long stairs and wait for the next bell, arrow, and stampede.

That evening I hustled down the steps with thirty or more people hoping to get on the train from Braintree. The crowd was moving fast as the train pulled into the station and the momentum behind me turned from push to shove. I felt two hands on my back, and one targeted shove hurled me out off the platform. I flailed my arms trying to right myself—trying to reverse my motion—but I landed on the track on my hands and knees. The gravel dug into my palms and one knee slammed hard into the rail. The smell of exhaust and fear stung my nose. I could hear the roar of the train coming and I turned. The headlight was close and blinded me for a moment. I blinked hard and gasped for clean air. I turned to see a man was reaching for me but I couldn't get his hand. Something wasn't right with my arm. Then the hands came closer and grabbed me. The train was screeching on the track trying to stop. The sound vibrated through my whole body and the bright light blinded me. I felt the hands pull and my body scraped up the edge of the platform. The screeching came louder. People were screaming. Two men pulled me up onto the platform. I sat up and looked at the tracks. The train had stopped twenty feet past where I'd been. A man in a uniform came rushing over. One of the men asked me if I was okay and I said I was.

"Thank you. I... did you see?... I, just thank you."

"I only saw you go over," one man said.

The other man nodded. "It was a pretty big crowd. I looked to see who had been right behind you but I couldn't tell."

"I don't know how to thank you." I tried to get up, but my left arm folded under when I leaned on it.

"Stay still, ma'am," the uniformed guy said. "There's more help coming."

He asked the two men to give statements and their contact information, and a couple of paramedics arrived with a stretcher.

"I'm not that bad," I objected. "I'm okay—dizzy. I can walk with some help."

They loaded me on the stretcher anyway and whisked me to Mass General, where they set my broken wrist. Toryn and Gloria arrived as if by magic. Or maybe I gave the ER attendant Gloria's number. Hard to remember.

On Saturday morning I woke up chilled and achy in general, and with wrist pain quite specifically. December had won the match and I was down for the count. I slept on and off all day, waking occasionally to listen to the pigeons ooorh-ing on the sill outside my window. My sleep was restless. I dreamt I was a child, but at the same time I was looking in on my childhood from the present. My family was staying with my grandparents in Minnesota and I saw the woods and the lake where we used to play. But something wasn't right. It felt as if I should treasure that time, that it should be special and nurturing, but it wasn't and I wanted to go back and make it right.

I woke in a sweat and had to sit up to catch my breath. The weird thing was that I consciously remembered very little of my childhood, but my mind could bring me vivid and specific memories, so it was all still stored there, just out of my reach. If it was still stored there, then it still mattered. I didn't like that fact.

I'd learned what looking back got me: it

got me caught back in the sticky web of what other people wanted me to be. As an adult I was fully independent; my parents had passed away, and my life was my own. But I was beginning to think it was time for the song to come to the bridge, because I'd created new problems in the process of escaping the old. I'd shut myself off from the possibility of ever being vulnerable and it's hard to have a relationship without opening up at least a little.

I thought about all the children I'd worked with over the years, and the adults dealing with issues from their childhoods. It was so much easier to know how to help them than myself.

I checked my phone. No message from Dani. Fragile from being sick and from all the vivid weird dreams, I became frantic about her. Was she safe? How would she salvage herself from her mother's death? All of Anita's good mothering could fall victim to that family mishandling Dani now.

I snuggled back under my quilt. Patchworked and floral, it looked like a grandma had made it, but it hadn't actually come to Boston in the U-Haul-of-hope with me. It was from Pottery Barn. I'd bought it that first winter when my hopes began to dim and I learned the depth of the Boston cold.

By Sunday afternoon I was feeling better and I called my brother, Owen, who had moved to Newport, New Hampshire, two years before. Owen was out with the kids feeding the alpacas on the farm that was his full-time job (along with raising four girls). I talked with his wife, Maria, who reported that the girls were doing well, the family had added a yellow Lab puppy, and Owen was continuing to enjoy his new life as a farmer and manager of all-things-girl. The notion of my little brother the jock as a full-time daddy playing princess and washing endless pairs of pink tights was an enormous amusement to me. Maria was a pediatrician, splitting her time between teaching at the Dartmouth med school and her practice in Newport, leaving Owen in charge at home. So far it seemed to suit him. I promised to visit soon and sent my love to Owen and the girls.

When I hung up I thought about how Owen had married a healer of children. We'd lost our sister twenty-five years before, but we were both trying to make up for so much. He was a great dad to four girls and I was trying to help other people's children. It was as if we were still trying to take care of Sarah: to show her, as she looked down from heaven, that we were still trying to make things better.

Weekends were busy times for Gloria at work, but when she got home Sunday evening she was hell-bent on cheering me up. She told me to get dressed, then went out to the living room and put on some Cuban jazz. She mixed a pitcher of margaritas. Toryn showed up with flowers and carry-out tacos.

After a margarita my arm stopped hurting and I totally enjoyed Toryn and Gloria's banter as they tried to up each other with stupid people stories from work.

"Guy called 911 to report that his wife stole his cocaine," Toryn said.

Gloria said, "Guy had a beer tap tattooed on his fat belly."

"Guy tried to rob a gun store using a baseball bat."

"Woman got her dimples pierced."

"Woman robbed a store wearing her GPS ankle bracelet."

I had some dumb people stories of my own from counseling, but they were the kind that tended to hit closer to home and were only funny if you were in the right mood.

I went to bed significantly cheered, if a little dizzy when I closed my eyes. As I lay there, hoping for sleep to come, it occurred to me that denial wasn't going to work. If someone was trying to kill me, I needed to know.

CHAPTER SEVEN

Monday came and still no word from Dani. I wanted to call but I was afraid to stir up more trouble with Dob. I had no idea if he was really trying to protect me from danger, trying to hide something, trying to kill me, or just weird. I was nervous leaving my apartment for the first time since I was pushed. I stayed hyperaware of people around me and speed-walked to work.

Then Toryn called. "Brian's in the hospital. He was hit by a car on Friday evening near the UMass campus."

"What?" A chill went through me and my arm throbbed. "What time?"

"Around six thirty. The police are looking for leads, but they don't have any witnesses. He hasn't regained consciousness."

"Are the police considering it connected to Anita's death?"

"I don't know, but they haven't confirmed that Anita's death wasn't accidental, so I doubt if they'll put a lot of resources into looking for links."

Toryn was at work and couldn't talk long, so we hung up and I tried to digest the news. I wanted to call Hank, but I couldn't. I wanted to talk to Dani and see how she was handling it, or if she'd even heard, but I couldn't.

That afternoon DCF called Vivian. She came to my office with the news. The child welfare visit had caught the Nayak family at a bad moment: both Dob and Josephine had been drinking, and Dani had her arm wrapped in bandages. The social worker insisted on seeing what Dob described as a cooking burn, and it wasn't a burn. Dani had carved "Mom" in her arm along with a heart. DCF called Dani's dad. He said he would come up as soon as he could get away. They were waiting to hear from him about when that would be.

"We did the right thing," Vivian said, her dark bob swinging with her declarative nod. "I know you'd rather help her yourself, but at least she'll be out of that house and you won't have the temptation to get overly involved."

"Yeah." I decided to let her jab go and focus on Dani. "And she'll be far away from her school, friends, and supports." There were only bad options at that point.

"She was successful with her cries for help. I'll make sure DCF here calls DCF in Philly to make them aware of the situation. They should set up some counseling for her there."

"Yeah." I felt like a sullen teenager myself with my monosyllabic responses to Vivian. A cramp tightened deep in my gut, a longing that reached back across my whole lifetime. I didn't know what it was like to lose a wonderful mom, but I knew what it was like to long deeply for one. You could get money later in life, friends, success, skills—there were all sorts of things a person could create for themselves in adulthood, but not a childhood with a loving mom.

I can't do this job anymore, I thought. *Nothing I do helps.* But even as I had the thought, I kind of didn't believe myself because I'd seen how counseling helped people. I believed that Vivian and Nathan had made positive impacts on people's lives. But it felt like it was costing me too much to try.

"Penny, you do know that nobody is able to help every client as much as they'd like." I braced for the rest of what she had to say. "You're going to have to develop a thicker skin." *There it was.* "If you fall apart over one client, what about the rest of them? Were you this soft-hearted at Juvenile Probation? Is that why you burned out? You'll burn out here too if you get overly involved." I avoided her eyes because I was so angry and conflicted I thought I might cry.

I managed to say, "She needs help. That's what I'm supposed to do: help her. Talking with her an hour per week isn't solving her problems."

"Hear me, Penny, getting involved in a client's troubles to this extent is not acceptable as a social worker."

I texted Toryn to call me when he could. The phone rang a few minutes later. I told him about DCF's visit to Dani. "Where the hell is her dad? I need to know if she's okay, Tor."

"You're not going there."

"I am."

He sighed. "Then I'm going with you."

The rest of the afternoon crawled by.

Finally the clock struck five and I was out the door. I was scared to get back on the T, so I stood back against the wall while I waited for the train, then ran to get on when it stopped at the platform. Inside, I was crammed in near full-body contact with loud, smelly teenagers. I watched commuters, crabby and worn out from their jobs. I was grateful that I didn't have a commute. A lot of these people rode the T to a commuter train and took that to their car. It could easily be an hour and a half each way. That was three hours each day when they weren't cooking or walking in the park or playing Chutes and Ladders with the kids. Fifteen hours each week when they could be learning to speak Mandarin or taking a printmaking class or coaching third grade soccer.

The subway air was thick and warm, but I emerged into a biting cold. Toryn and I met just outside the station and walked over the freeway and up the hill to the Nayaks' house. I didn't know what I was going to say when we got there and I didn't care.

I rang the bell. We waited. It was crazy cold and darkness was closing in. The only sounds were distant traffic noises and a lonely dog barking. Toryn was tapping his foot. I narrowed my eyes at him and he stopped. I listened but didn't hear anything inside. They probably forbade Dani from answering the door. I rang again. The wind kicked up and Toryn and I both shoved our hands in our pockets and bowed our heads against the briny cold.

"They're not here, Penny, we should

go."

"I'm not leaving. I'll wait." I looked around for a spot to sit it out. The choices were cold cement and icy brown grass.

Just then, a black Lexus pulled up and parked, rims scraping loudly on the curb. Dob Nayak flung himself out and slammed the door.

"What the hell are you doing here?" he spat.

"DCF reported back after their visit, Mr. Nayak. You aren't taking care of her. I want to see her."

"She isn't here."

"Where is she?"

"Why would I tell you that? Stay out of our business." Toryn bumped me and looked to the street where a police cruiser was pulling up to the curb. Dob smirked. "I called the police when I saw you at the door. I hope this will help you take my request more seriously."

I felt like a truant schoolgirl as I watched the skinny cop walk toward us, but I recognized that particular heart-pounding as my overreaction to authority. I wasn't giving up so easily. Dob was in the wrong, not me.

"We got a call," the skinny cop barked as he approached. "How can I help?" His cowboy walk and loud voice failed to make up for his small stature.

"I've asked this woman to leave my young niece and our family alone, but she continually harasses us. I'd like her removed from my property and I plan to file a restraining order."

The cop turned his hard gaze to me. I

guessed he was new by how seriously he seemed to take himself. "Your name, ma'am?"

Before I could answer, his big black partner got out of the car and said, "Penny? What's up, girl?" He glanced at my arm. "You okay?"

It was a cop I knew when I worked Juvenile. We'd worked together in defense of kids a number of times.

"Duane, great to see you. I'm checking on one of my clients. Her uncle doesn't want the interference, but DCF found him and his wife drunk and the girl with self-harm. I haven't heard from her and I want to make sure she's okay."

"She's not here," Dob shouted. "Now get out of here."

I'd succeeded in embarrassing him. Too bad he didn't have the sense to just be decent in the first place.

"Sir, can you tell us where your niece is now?" Duane asked. The other cop just stood there with one hip jutted out and a bad attitude on his face.

"She is at an event at her school. Thank you for coming, officers. Goodbye."

He fumbled with the lock then dashed into the house. We regrouped on the sidewalk at the street. "New job same shit?" Duane asked.

"Pretty much. Thanks for being on the beat, Duane. You're a welcome sight."

"Lemme know what ya need."

"Can you come by later and make sure Dani is okay?"

Duane promised to check on her and

left me with a one-armed shoulder hug and a sympathetic smile.

My return trip on the T was less crowded but I was still nervous in the station and I stayed far from the tracks.

At home I took some ibuprofen for my throbbing arm, then emailed Will.

I had this client, Dani. I really wanted to help her. Her mom died—maybe was murdered. She is really struggling and has to move to Philly to be with her dad, who has never been much of a dad. I'm having a hard time with it all.

Ten minutes after I sent the email, my phone rang.

"Penny, it's me. Your note sounded like you could use a friend."

I hadn't heard his voice in nearly a year. Relief and nervousness combined to leave me confused, but I managed to say, "Wow. That's really nice of you, I guess you're right. It's been a rough few weeks."

"Tell me."

So I did. We talked for over an hour and I found myself comforted by being able to share the whole story with someone who knows me so well. I didn't have to explain why I'd gotten so personally involved or why I couldn't just let it go. I didn't tell him about the subway incident, though, because I didn't want him to get all worried and overprotective.

When Gloria got home from work I told her what was happening. She jumped right in and hatched a plan to shadow Josephine and find out who her young mystery lover was.

"It's unbelievable what we overhear at the spa. It's like we're invisible. Anyway, maybe we'll learn something interesting. I wouldn't be surprised if Josephine was part of something shady. We can just hang down in Government Center near her building and see where she goes. We should probably wear hats or something, but it's damn cold, so we can bundle up and she'll never see us."

"Kind of crazy, don't ya think, Gloria?" But I had to admit I was curious. Poor Dani was living in a household with the Hell Boar and the Shady Adulteress. I wanted to know all I could about them. "But I guess we have every right to hang out downtown and just happen to walk the same way she does after work."

Duane called at ten o'clock and said he'd checked in and Dani wasn't back at the Nayaks yet. "I'm sorry I can't do more. They say she's at a friend's house in Cambridge and it's out of my jurisdiction. I have to take them at their word."

I thanked him for checking, and asked him to let me know if he learned anything else.

Worry made me nauseous but I couldn't blame Dani for wanting to stay away from the house of cold evil.

CHAPTER EIGHT

I muddled through Tuesday by telling myself that Dani was fine, and it was probably really nice for her to spend some time with friends, away from Dob and Josephine. Whoever killed her mom and hit Brian, and maybe pushed me onto the subway tracks, wouldn't have an interest in hurting her. She wasn't snooping or getting into trouble.

Gloria and I met at five outside of Josephine's building. Gloria hid her big hair under a wooly knit cap and I pulled my hair back and put my hood up. We both wrapped scarves around our faces and tried to act inconspicuous. It was cold, my arm ached, and we waited a long time, standing in the plaza. The people-watching was good, though, and a Clover Food truck came by, so we had good eats. The whole PI thing seemed almost appealing.

After about an hour we noticed there was a guy who had been lurking there a long time too. He glanced at us from time to time, just as we did him. "Do you think we're being followed?" I asked Gloria.

"Why in the world would someone follow us? To steal my aromatherapy formulas? Or are you in some kind of mysterious trouble?"

"No, very funny, but I don't know. It's just kind of creepy."

I saw the man look up and turn to watch a guy in his mid-twenties wearing dressy jeans and a leather jacket enter the building. The man was only there a moment and left. The lurker guy followed him and Gloria and I glanced at each other and followed the lurker.

"We'll stay in sight of the building," she said, "but let's see where they're going."

We didn't have to follow far. The young man stepped into a pub less than a block away. We found a spot to sit where we could see down the street in both directions. Moments later, Josephine emerged from her building. The lurker was about twenty feet from us, and like us he'd kept an eye on her building. He watched her. She headed in our direction and Gloria and I stepped into a convenience store until she passed. She went into the pub. We waited. Lurker waited. We watched Lurker. He watched us. We were cold and nervous and not having fun.

"Do you think Dob hired someone to watch Jo? Maybe he knows about the affair," Gloria said.

"God, all hell could break loose at the Nayaks'. Poor Dani!"

I burrowed down into my jacket a bit and rewrapped my scarf. Will had given me that scarf years ago and it was still my favorite.

"Gloria, tell me how you manage the whole love life thing."

"I attract them with my beauty and intelligence." She smiled.

"Yeah, but how do you keep yourself out there? I saw you when it didn't work out with Mark. You were devastated. But you didn't give up on men."

"Giving up on men wouldn't be fun," she said. "Penny, this is my advice and the advice of my foremothers: you have to be willing to bleed."

I cocked my head, waiting for that to sink in.

She continued. "If you like a guy enough to be terrified of what will happen if it doesn't work out, that's not the guy to throw away. You accept that your chance at happiness comes with an equal or greater chance of pain." She watched as Lurker paced nearby. "You'll probably have both."

It sounded wise, maybe because it was suspiciously serious for Gloria.

We waited and watched the pub. The street was fairly busy so when the hand landed on my back at first I thought I was jostled by a passerby. But the hand stayed and Gloria's eyes grew wide looking over my shoulder. I froze.

"Are you waiting for Mrs. Nayak?"

I turned. He was sandy brown and average looking, if bulky.

"Uh, we—" Gloria stammered, "we're just worried about her, so we were sort of checking on her."

"Oh, did she already know what Robby wanted to tell her?"

"Uh—" My jaw relaxed a bit. "Robby?"

"Yeah, he's telling his mom he's gay. He's going to come out and get me when he's ready to introduce me. We're getting married." He smiled and blushed.

"Congratulations!" I smiled back at him. "Do you think it will go well in there?"

"Say a little prayer?"

The man in the leather jacket opened the pub door and looked out. I winked at our new friend and Gloria and I turned toward the Downtown Crossing T station.

"Huh," she said, "wait 'til I tell the estheticians. It's a big wager pool."

I turned to look at her, speechless. I remembered that our information was completely based on spa gossip. I did a mental head slap.

"I had money on the landscaper. Do you think having an affair with her gay son is close enough?"

Wednesday morning Duane called to tell me that when he got on his shift he found an APB for Dani. Her dad had arrived from Philly, and Dob and Jo didn't actually know where she was. They claimed she was having another overnight with a girlfriend, but Chris couldn't reach her and she hadn't been to school since Monday.

I didn't know what to do. I wanted to look for her, but I had to keep my job, and I was certain that if I walked out I'd be fired.

I figured it was futile but I texted her anyway.

Me: Where are you?

I hung in and saw my clients. I was

distracted and jittery, maybe the worst counseling professional on the face of the earth, but I stayed until the last client was gone. Then I went directly to Toryn's apartment.

Toryn was already in pajama pants. Soft jazz played on the stereo and he had his collection of old-fashioned wind-up toys strewn across the living area. "Semiannual cleaning," he said. He looked me up and down and said, "Those are some kick-ass new shit-stomping boots!"

I smiled just a little, more pleased at his approval than I wanted to let on. "Tor, I need to borrow your car, pretty please." I was talking fast and breathing hard. Hives itched from my neck to my waist. I explained what Duane had told me. "If I were her I'd hide out at her old apartment. I want to stake it out."

Tor went to his tiny kitchen and pulled out a cloth grocery bag. He started loading it with crackers, chips, cheese, and peanut butter. He pulled a couple of beers from the fridge and filled two Nalgene water bottles. I scratched and jittered. "Tor, I'm not going for a picnic. I need to hurry and find Dani!"

"Well, you're not going alone, and I'm gonna get hungry. You'll thank me later."

I did.

We parked Toryn's old Mercedes on the street outside the apartment. The best spot we could find didn't give us a perfect view, but it was good enough. At first it seemed kind of exciting to be on a stakeout, and Toryn's car was pretty comfortable. But we didn't want to leave the car running, so it got really cold and we stood it as long as we could before running the engine a little to warm it back up.

"Stop scratching!" Toryn groused after a while.

"I can't help it!" I pulled up my shirt to reveal the splotches on my tummy.

"Ew. Be careful not to flash me any girl parts—they're as bad as hives!"

"Well, I guess you're lucky your mama had them."

"Go get some cream."

I got out of the car and started walking. I hoped he'd think I was huffy, but I itched something fierce and getting cream was a good idea.

I returned to the car twenty minutes later with a tube of hydrocortisone, some dark chocolate, two bottles of iced latte, two more beers, Fritos, Fun-Yums, Bit-o-Honey, and Tums.

Toryn grabbed a beer, but I'd gotten an import, and we didn't have an opener. Toryn turned off the car and set to work on the cap with a key.

We talked about Brian's "accident" and Anita's murder and fingered absolutely everyone as the killer, but didn't convince ourselves of anyone. The snacks lost their entertainment value and the cold and boredom made us crabby.

Toryn worked on the beer all the while.

"That key isn't looking good," I observed.

"That's okay, it's just my neighbor's apartment key. Cats can go like a week without food, right?"

We made up a game where one person would say a line from a movie and the other would try to think of the closest matching line from a song. When that got old, we took turns watching the building while the other person played games on their phone. When our batteries were too low, we made up another song lyric game but it was stupid and we ended up arguing over the rules.

Around one in the morning I suggested we give up. "Wherever she is, she's sound asleep by now," I reasoned. Toryn agreed and drove me home. I slunk into my building a complete failure.

CHAPTER NINE

Dani finally called on Friday. She reached me just as I was leaving the office after another day of bad social work.

"Where are you?" I took my first deep breath all day.

"I'm fine, Penny."

"No, Dani, everyone is looking for you. Including the police! Please tell me where you are and why you ran off and I'll figure out how to help you."

"Penny, I'm okay. I had to get out of there and I don't want to go to Philly. I can take care of myself."

I was walking up the sidewalk outside the office, and I stopped to sit on a door stoop so I could focus. The cold of the concrete went right through my pants, and I wondered if she was cold where she was.

"I know you can take care of yourself, Dani. But I want to help you, okay?"

I crossed the fingers of my frozen left hand. I hadn't been able to get a glove over the cast.

"I know. Thanks, Penny. The thing is..." Her voice sounded choked and I started to sweat. "On Monday I found out Brian had been hit by a car. Then DCF came to the house and said I had to go with my dad as soon as he could get here." She sniffled and went on. "Whoever killed Mom is out there, and the police are stupid, and there's no way I'm going to Philly where I can't even look for her killer!"

I stood up and started walking. Dani continued, "So I took off." I waited. "Then today I went to Boston Medical Center to see Brian and he's dead!" She was crying. It took me a moment to absorb the news, then I felt like crying too, whether out of sadness or fear I couldn't say.

When we'd both calmed ourselves a little I said, "I'm so sorry. It's so awful I don't even know what to say." I didn't want to scare her more, but I had to get her someplace safe. "Do you understand that I'm concerned about you? You can't go looking for a murderer alone!"

"I know who did it, Penny. It was Thomas. He and Mom were always fighting about how the business should be run and he wanted to take over, but Harry wanted Mom to take over. I bet her computer was there, and the family gems were in the safe."

I was a block from Anita's apartment and walking fast.

She went on, "Brian knew about their arguments, and he must have known it was Thomas, so Thomas killed him too."

"Wow, have you talked to Hank about this?"

"No. I can't call him with everyone looking for me."

I was in sight of the apartment, but it didn't seem like a good time to tell her I was there after her last comment. I slowed in case she was peeking out the window around the drawn shades. "You know, I'm good at asking questions. Do you want to pay a visit to Thomas?" Crap, the words came out before I could think about how stupid that was. I just wanted to get my hands on her.

"I do!" she replied. "Will you really help me?"

"Dani, I'm at the apartment now. Will you let me in and we can talk about how to do this?" The window shade moved a little and I walked up to the door.

"What happened to your arm?" she asked when she opened the door.

"I'm super clumsy is all. I fell and broke it a little, but it's fine."

She had her coat on and was ready to go, but I asked to use the bathroom. While I was in there I texted Hank.

Me: Found Dani.
Meet us at Mt. V. Jewel asap?

I blew my nose, which was constantly running from the cold, and when I tossed the tissue in the trash I saw it. A condom box. I felt like someone had punched me in the gut. I'd just secured her trust and retrieved her from being missing. There was no way I could confront this yet.

Twenty minutes later we were crammed onto the T, squished into seats next to each other. It was still rush hour and normally we'd never get even one seat, so it was bad luck that we'd gotten two and I couldn't check my phone to see if Hank had gotten the message. Dani talked nonstop.

"Dob told me that I couldn't call or text you. He was checking my phone and said if I deleted the history he'd find it on the bill anyway and he would cancel my phone. It got really weird there." She paused to watch the jostling at the South Station stop, then went on, "I think the cops were watching for me at Mom's apartment, so I didn't use any lights or turn the heat up or anything. I had to check the street if I went out, so I stayed in the apartment a lot. It's been really freaky and cold, but at least my dad can't drag me to Philly."

I tried to listen to everything Dani wanted to tell me, but I needed to think through a plan to keep us both safe and deliver Dani to Hank. I hoped Harry would be at the shop and not Thomas. Maybe Harry could distract Dani for a while and give Hank time to get there.

We arrived at Charles MGH station and started our descent of Beacon Hill. Our walk was silent, and when we reached the shop Dani turned and looked at me with big, frightened eyes. She straightened and took a big breath, then opened the door.

Thomas was there, and Harry was not. "Dani, Penny, nice to see you," he said. "I was just closing up for the evening." He walked around us, flipped the "open" sign to "closed," and locked the door.

I glanced at the clock on the wall. It had been about a half hour since I texted Hank and it would take him at least an hour to get in from Wayland, if he even got my text and came.

Dani was silent and Thomas was regarding us with what I assumed was curiosity, but he was so dull and expressionless by nature that I had to just guess. I couldn't imagine such a dud working up the passion to murder someone, let alone two people. But then I remembered his angry voice coming from the back of the shop when he was on the phone that time. Maybe he was a Jekyll and Hyde type.

"I hope we aren't keeping you from something." I tried to sound light and friendly. I hoped he couldn't hear the tremor in my voice. "Dani was feeling really down so I suggested we come by to see Harry. He always cheers her up."

"I'm sorry. Dad's not here. He left for home about an hour ago."

Dani spoke up. "Thomas, I was wondering if some of Mom's stuff might still be here. My uncle and I boxed up most of the apartment for storage, but I didn't think about her stuff in her desk here or whatever."

"Oh, of course," he said slowly. "We haven't really done much with her desk. Do you want to take a look and see if there's anything you want to keep?" He gestured his head toward the back room. I felt sweat stinging the hives on my back. I reminded myself to breathe, and unclenched my hands long enough to take my one glove off.

Dani was forging ahead as if we weren't locked in a dark store with a possible murderer, as if she wasn't the timid shy child I'd met a couple of weeks ago. She followed Thomas to the back. I glanced at the door, but when Thomas turned to see if I was coming, I took a few steps in their direction. I wanted to keep Dani in sight, but also be in range of the door.

"Mom didn't want the shop to sell anything but fair trade gems, right?"

I couldn't believe what Dani was doing, but at the same time, we came for a reason and she had questions. I hoped she wasn't opening up something explosive.

"That's right," Thomas replied, failing to mask the annoyance in his voice, "but the shop has barely turned a profit over the past five years. People are less discriminating when the economy is unsure."

"So, will you take over now?" she asked. My breath was shallow. I wondered if oxygen was getting to my brain.

"My dad is still working," he said. "We'll work together for now. Why all the questions about the business, Dani?" Thomas was standing right over her as she rummaged through the drawers of Anita's desk. She turned and looked up at him and I saw a flash of fear in her eyes. She turned back to the piles she was making on the desk. A hairbrush, a bunch of Chapsticks, some snack bars, hand sanitizer, an old cell phone. She found a moleskin notebook and flipped through it.

"Mom had sketches like this everywhere," she said. And as if to prove her point she pulled a cocktail napkin from between the pages and held up a sketch of what looked like a studded choker with a leash. She tucked it back into the book and put the book in her "keep" pile.

Thomas had disappeared farther into the back of the shop. I turned to look for him, but a tall set of shelves blocked my view. I decided to get Dani out of there before he came back.

A loud thud made us jump. I turned to see Hank at the door. I dove for the handle, unlocked the deadbolt, and let him in.

Dani came out of the back room right behind Thomas. She looked relieved when she saw Hank, but her expression changed quickly and she shot me a hurt, accusing look.

Hank greeted Thomas, explaining that Dani had been missing and I'd texted him to meet us there. I stepped closer to Dani and whispered, "I thought we might need backup."

"I was downtown at headquarters," Hank said, "about the investigation into Brian's death."

I hoped he would stop talking to Thomas. He had no idea of Dani's suspicions. What if she was right?

"Dani," Thomas said quietly, "just in case you are wondering about me, the police have confirmed that I was here when your mom died and when Brian was hit." It was the most expression I'd seen on his face. "Maybe you'll let me be a friend? I'll help if I can."

Dani was silent.

Finally Hank spoke. "Dani, I'm taking you home to Wayland with me."

Dani pleaded, "Uncle Hank, my dad is trying to take me to Philly. I can't leave Boston!"

He took her by the arm in a no-discussion manner and led her to the door. "We'll invite your dad over to talk, and Jenny and I will persuade him to let you stay with us."

The three of us left the store and said brief goodbyes on the street. I watched them pull away from the curb and started my trek home with a relieved little kick in my shit-stompin' boots.

"Oh, crap, that's Jill." I grabbed Gloria's arm too late. Jill was nearly on top of us, having appeared suddenly out of the jazz club crowd. She was all cleavage and shimmer, and I wondered how she could balance her top half on those skinny legs and stiletto heels.

Gloria had held me to our plans to go out that night, so I'd done a quick change and headed back out the door.

"Oh, hi. Penny, right?" Jill smiled a crooked smile at me, then squinted at Gloria. "And aren't you the manager at the spa?" Gloria smiled a customer service smile. "I thought you lived out of town," she said, turning back to me.

Gloria jumped in a little too loudly, but the band was playing and the place was packed. "She's staying with me for a while. We're old friends from school. I'm trying to convince her to move here."

Jill's suspicious expression didn't budge, but she lightened her voice. I held my broken arm behind me. "How's Dani?" she asked. "Is she still staying with Dob?"

"She's with the Dorians for now," I said. "I heard they've opened an investigation into how Anita died. I always told her not to keep the big jewelry at home. Did they find evidence of robbery?"

"I don't know," I said. "Did she keep stuff like that at home?"

"She used to. The pieces from her grandfather were worth hundreds of thousands of dollars. I begged her to put them someplace safe, but she told me to butt out."

Jill waved at someone over my shoulder. "Gotta go. Take care." She bumped off through the crowd.

I let out the breath I'd been holding. I'd agreed to come out with Gloria to get my mind off of Dani. I slugged my wine.

Gloria pointed at two little tables, each with one empty chair. Worth a shot. The guy at one table offered his up, but the woman at the other was saving hers for someone, so I wandered around until I found a spare chair to bring over. The second guy at the table Gloria had joined made room for me next to him. I smiled to thank him. When we made eye contact I felt a funny skip-thud in my chest. I wondered if they were circulating fresh air into the bar. "I'm Marco Lang." Hint of an accent I couldn't place.

"Penny Wade. Nice to meet you." I realized I was still standing. I sat. He scooched his chair to make more room for me next to him so I'd be facing the band. I scooched. We watched. He smelled like balsam soap.

When the band finished the song and paused, I leaned over. "So you like jazz. Do you play?"

My gaze stopped on his beautiful, beautiful mouth. I watched it as he replied. "I do a little. Do you?"

"No, I wish I did."

The band started up again, melodic and silky. Gloria glanced over from across the table and smiled without betraying any trace of "you landed next to a God," but I knew what she was thinking.

Marco bought a round for the table. When I leaned in to thank him over the noise, he casually put his hand on my arm. I was glad he was on my right. The room was warm and I started to sweat a little.

My third glass of wine made the lights and music magical. I decided that glass would be my last. This guy was so handsome that he probably found a new girl nightly. I tensed at the thought and turned back to watch the band. I would leave when the band took a break.

I listened to several more songs, enjoying the music and the distraction from worry about Dani. Marco's presence was strong next to me.

"You said you wished you played. What would you play if you could?" He'd leaned in close and I smelled the clean, woodsy scent again.

"Piano."

"Mmm. You could learn, you know."

"I'm not so sure. What do you play?"

"I mostly focus on the guitar, but some other strings too, and I like hand drums."

I knew that if I kept looking at him my brain would dissolve like warm Jell-O and my body would start making decisions. I shored myself up. "That's cool." I turned back to the band.

When the break came I was reluctant to leave, but determined to save myself from Casanova. I told Gloria I was leaving. Marco stood and walked around the table to meet Gloria. Marco flashed her a short, high-wattage smile and Gloria glanced demurely to the floor before raising her eyes to him.

"Nice to meet you. Thanks for the drink."

"My pleasure, Gloria."

I felt like I'd faded into the crowd.

"So you two are roommates?" he asked.

I could imagine what was going through his head.

"We are." Gloria giggled. Was she reading his mind too? We definitely did not come as a set! I was about to just back out of the club and leave the two of them to their flirting when he turned back to me.

I said, "Thanks for the drink. I need to go."

The corners of his mouth turned down a little but his eyes stayed bright. "Penny Wade, will you join me at Bristol for brunch on Sunday? There's a pianist you should see."

I hesitated. I loved the Four Seasons with the Bristol's huge windows looking out on the Public Garden. But I'd told myself to steer clear of this guy and I needed to stick to my sanity.

"Okay," he said, "I see you're hesitant and I know you don't really know me. I'm going to be at Bristol listening to outstanding piano music on Sunday at ten—alone unless you choose to join me. I'm not trying to give you guilt, I often eat breakfast with the *New York Times* for company and am quite content. But if you join me, I'll be very pleased." He smiled and my stomach jumped.

"It is a very nice offer." I'd planned to turn him down flat but I failed. "I'll give it some thought when my head is clearer."

On Saturday I did some research on Chris. The Google search of his name got me a bunch of mug shots, some athletes, a surprising number of priests, and a photo of a guy playing the mandolin in the center of a gigantic aloe plant. I couldn't identify him on LinkedIn or Facebook.

Dani had told me a little about him. He grew up in Florida and moved to Boston for college. While he and Anita were married he worked at various sales jobs: mattresses, cars, above-ground pools. Dani remembered him with a beer in hand after work, watching sports on TV and arguing with her mom.

With a bit more searching, I found his business, Ruby Road, an overwhelming and disorganized website that appeared to sell almost everything cheap. While it clearly tried to effect an exotic look, it succeeded about as well as the torn and curled posters you see in cheap Indian restaurants did at invoking the mystic ambience of India.

In the clothing menu, there were saris, shawls, and scarves. There were Indian print shirts and tunics for men and T-shirts with pictures of Buddhas. There were dozens of handbags, wallets, and briefcases. In addition to the clothing, there were menus of toys, sweets, and crafts.

I hadn't really learned anything about Chris and I didn't even know what I was looking for. I just knew that when the cops look for murderers on TV, they always look at partners and ex-partners first.

Gloria skipped into the apartment close to noon. She sang "High Flying, Adored" from *Evita* as she put on a pot of coffee.

"Seriously, Gloria, I'm glad it's going well with Anton, but be careful. Eva Perón fell from those heights, remember?"

I started singing "Another Suitcase in Another Hall."

She sang the chorus from "Rainbow High," then leaned on the breakfast bar where I was sitting on the other side. "It's been four months," she said. "You need to take your suitcase into another bedroom. Maybe you'll land back out in another hall, nobody ever knows that, but *David wasn't the one*."

Nobody had dared to mention David since I'd gotten through the darkest part and resurfaced a couple of months before. I cringed with loss at the sound of his name. I didn't want to talk about it and I didn't know if I could move on or whether there was something I was still supposed to sort out or process or whatever.

"I'm not like you," I said. "I don't just bounce back. I'm still devastated that he didn't want me, that I could be so in love with someone who couldn't or wouldn't return it."

"*Ay, dios mio*. David was a Pisces. It's

the sign of self-undoing. There are two fish in the symbol for a reason—there's just a whole lot going on with those guys. But Marco's a Scorpio."

"What?" I cut her off. "How do you know?"

"I asked him after you left."

"You asked him his *sign*?"

"No, I asked him his birthday, but he probably knew why. No matter, though. Scorpios are the very most passionate men under their cool, charming exteriors. They're dangerous and mysterious and in Marco's case, *totally* hot!"

I didn't know whether to listen to or dismiss her. Would I really evaluate a guy based on astrology?

"You're going out with him tomorrow, right?"

"I haven't decided."

"No problem. I decided for you. You're going."

CHAPTER TEN

"I've ordered two mimosas." Marco smiled as he rose to pull out my chair. The waitress was just leaving the table as I arrived; I'd seen her flirting with Marco as I crossed the restaurant. I was already cursing myself. I had no business dating a guy that attracted every pretty woman in Boston. But I'd hopped out of bed that morning, dressed carefully, and my legs had brought me here.

"I'm glad you came," he said as he sat back down with his back to the Public Garden, giving me the view. But the view of Marco was even better: milk chocolate cashmere sweater, thick wavy almost-black hair. He was clean shaven, but even so I could see the dark shadow of his beard.

"Thanks for inviting me." My mouth was a little dry, so I reached for my water glass, being extra careful not to knock it over.

Marco smiled and nodded toward the piano. "She should be starting soon. You won't be disappointed. In the meantime, I've ordered a fruit plate to share, but look and see what else you'd like." He tapped his own menu and I opened mine, glad for the chance to break eye contact and breathe.

The waitress brought coffee, mimosas,

and a gorgeous platter of fruit. Marco told her we needed a little time to decide. I needed more than that—breakfast could be anything, but what was I doing here with him? I fidgeted with my napkin.

I ordered a bagel with lox, thinking it didn't indicate my feelings for Marco one way or another.

My phone rang. "So sorry." I dug it out of my bag to turn off the ringer but saw that it was Hank. "Oh, excuse me just a sec." I stood and answered, walking out to the lobby.

"Hi, Hank, sorry about that, I had to get to a quiet spot."

"I called to thank you. That was great work finding Dani. I also want to apologize. I talked with her and learned how Dob has been acting. He's clearly struggling, and he was out of line in how he treated both Dani and you. I know it doesn't excuse anything, but Dob was only fourteen when their mom passed away, and now he's lost his only sibling too."

"How's Dani doing?" I felt awkward standing in the big marble lobby of the Four Seasons and I hated being rude to Marco, but reminded myself that this date wasn't leading anywhere anyway.

"That's the other thing I want to tell you. Chris came over yesterday and we all talked. Jenny and I did our best to make the case for Dani to stay with us, but I'm afraid we didn't prevail. She and Chris went to Dob's to pack her things this morning, and they'll be on the road soon."

As upsetting as it was to have her leave, I wondered if it would be best to have a little distance from the boy with the condoms. I had a lot of questions for Hank but I didn't want to be rude to Marco any longer, so I had to choose carefully.

"Hank, um, did Dani tell you her suspicions about Thomas?"

"She did. Her stubborn involvement is the one good reason to have her in Philly. Penny, the police are on it. You and Dani took a risk on Friday. If Dani had been right, that could have been dangerous."

I didn't have time for a lecture so I tried to wrap up. "I hear you, Hank. Can we stay in touch?"

The pianist was playing when I returned to the table and Marco looked relaxed sitting in the morning light with his coffee in hand.

"I'm so sorry. It was about one of my clients—well, an ex-client, who's in a bad situation. I'm trying to track on her safety."

"So tell me about what you do."

I explained my new job, and my old one, and how stressful the transition to CCS had been, including the Dani story. I watched his reactions carefully, assessing whether he would judge me a bleeding heart, but he was interested. He didn't even pick up his fork. I was flattered, but really couldn't think what he wanted from me—aside from the obvious, of course—but that couldn't be in short supply for him.

"Do you think the job is sustainable for you? You seem passionate about it."

"I do. In some ways it's better than Juvie. There all my clients were in trouble and on the defensive. They hardly stood a fighting chance in the homes they came from and it was hard to make progress. We ended up monitoring them more than really helping them. There were exceptions, of course, but in a lot of ways we were set up to fail just by being part of a system that was punishing them for trying to survive as best they knew how."

"It sounds like you have high expectations for yourself. Who takes care of you while you take care of our city's youth?"

The guy was too smooth. I shrugged off his question and speared a strawberry. "I think it's worth it, most days. I hope being at CCS really will be better though."

"And your arm? Was that a job-related injury?"

"Just your garden variety accident," I fibbed.

He smiled, one corner of his mouth at a time.

In the office on Monday I kept the wheels in motion to see what I could learn about Chris. I called Toryn for the favor of checking background on Chris and the Nayaks. I called Harry to see if I could stop by after work. For the rest of the day, I did my real job.

I arrived at Mt. Vernon Jewelers around five thirty. Harry had tea ready and a hug for me. Thomas was there, talking to a customer about engagement rings. As Harry poured tea and fussed with cups and cookies, I got a snippet of an education about the quality and cuts of diamonds.

Harry hadn't heard from Dani, so I filled him in on her move to Philly, which gave me the opening I needed.

"Did you know Chris well? I know Dani doesn't have much of a relationship with him and I'm just wondering what he's like."

"Oh, I knew him well enough, I suppose. Never knew what Anita saw in him though. He was a bit of a ne'er-do-well. She figured that out eventually."

"Do you know much about his business? Or how his relationship was with Anita in recent years?"

"He's in the mooching business. He made contacts through Anita's dad and tried to gain his customers when he retired. He has some clothing and home décor and general junk."

"Dani overheard him complain to Dob that Anita had tried to ruin his business. Do you know what that might have been about? I thought they weren't in much contact."

"No, I don't know. I know Anita was bothered by the way he ran his business. She said that his online store was cheap and ugly and made India look bad. It got under her skin, I think, because Chris had spun his business off from her father's, which was a business of high integrity, of course." He sipped his tea then continued. "I don't know what he's got stuck in his craw from the divorce. It certainly wasn't amicable at the time. In any case, they would fight periodically over the years, although it became less frequent over time." He looked into his tea as he stirred it. "Anita was young when they met and she was ready to be free from her family. Indian families, especially Indian fathers, can be, well, highly involved. Anita had a more modern approach to womanhood than her father would have liked."

"Did she and her dad get along?" I asked.

"I'd say in the big picture they did, but it sounded to me like she needed to break free when she was in her twenties. That's when she met Chris. He was in the right place at the right time."

Had he been in the right place at the right time the night she died too?

CHAPTER ELEVEN

Dani was out of reach, there was no progress on the murders, work was touchy, and I was feeling distracted and insecure about Marco. Maybe I'd just run out of energy, maybe I was having seasonal affective disorder. Maybe I needed exercise.

Gloria got home around seven and found me in a fetal position on the couch. I hadn't turned on any lights despite the December evening gloom. I hadn't considered dinner or showering or anything really. She set down her stuff, put her hands on her hips, and tilted her head.

"I've made zero progress helping Dani and probably ruined my new job in the process," I explained.

She sat, then she stood. She went to her bag, grabbed her phone, and dialed. "Come over."

She hung up and took her bag of groceries into the kitchen and rustled around. She emerged with a glass of red Zinfandel and some crackers. I sipped and munched while she busied herself in the kitchen some more. Soon there were good smells, and the doorbell. She intercommed down and buzzed Toryn in.

Gloria had left the living room lights off out of respect for my self-pity. Toryn took one look and said, "God clearly forgot you when she called for light." I didn't answer. "But not when she said *Let there be delicious smells.* Gloria, did you invite me to eat or to drag Penny from the underworld?"

"Both," Gloria called from the kitchen. "I can't manage her on my own."

"Ah, barter," he replied. "I take care of Penny and you feed me." He walked over to the arm of the couch where I was propped and he lifted my weight off the arm and slid into my spot. He resettled me across him so I was supported by the couch arm again, across his lap.

I kept staring into nowhere. I pointed to my wine, an offering. "Yes, thank you," he said to me and then, "Waitress? A round for the couch please?" Gloria brought a glass for Toryn and a top-off for me.

He handed me my glass and we toasted. "To Dani," Toryn said.

"To Dani."

We were silent for a while, fading with the light, smelling garlic and mushrooms from the kitchen.

Finally Toryn said, "You can't save the world, Penny, or even just the children. But I'll do what I can to help you save Dani."

"Thanks."

"I've been a good snoop. Keeping an eye on things. I have some news."

I sat up and looked at him.

"Dob and Josephine are under investigation for money laundering," he said.

"Nothing conclusive, but their accounts are under review."

"What do the Nayaks do?"

"She works in a brokerage firm downtown, and together they own sort of an art dealership."

"I'd have guessed that they disdained art," I commented.

"Maybe they do, but they know it's worth money."

"So what is a 'sort-of' art dealership?"

"I'm not sure, but they don't have a gallery or anything and they seem to work within an established network of buyers and sellers. Art, cultural artifacts. Sort of diverse."

"So Dob and Josephine are doing something they need to hide?"

"Might be. It was the investigation of Anita's death that brought them to the attention of the police. There's a lot of process involved in a money laundering investigation. It could be a while before we know more."

Gloria came into the room with plates, napkins, and silverware and set the round table that sat between the kitchen and the living area. Then she brought out steaming bowls and a plate of flatbread.

"Dinner," she said.

Gloria had made mushroom curry, chana masala, and aloo paratha. A jar of lime pickle made busy rounds between us.

"Thank you for dinner, Gloria," I said. "It's amazing! Did you pin the recipes on Pinterest?"

"I did," she replied, smiling.

Gloria was starting a pretty amazing

recipe collection and I planned to use it as my go-to when I had time to start cooking again. The three of us ate in happy silence for a few minutes.

Toryn finally broke the quiet. "We need a plan."

"Amen to that." Gloria agreed. "Penny has to shake the heartbreak."

"We are *not* talking about David," I said. "The only thing that can help me is helping Dani."

"Let's go down there," Gloria said. Toryn nodded. A big, single nod.

When Gloria and Toryn finished plotting, we had a plan to take the 8:40 train Saturday morning. I called Marco to cancel the dinner date we'd set for Saturday evening. I explained what was happening with Dani, and that Gloria, Toryn, and I were going to Philly.

"Let me call you back," was all he said.

My heart dropped. I guess I blew that. Everything in my life was falling victim to this problem. But it was probably just as well. Marco probably couldn't be trusted anyway and I wasn't making the best decisions.

The phone rang before I could make it to the shower.

"I reserved three rooms at a B&B downtown. It belongs to some friends of mine. I'm coming with you."

I was taken aback by his boldness. How could he be so confident that I'd want him? And at the same time I felt a pulsing excitement that betrayed my attempts to resist his sexy charms.

On Saturday morning we all met at

South Station. Marco was gorgeous in a black leather jacket and jeans. He'd grown a short beard, maybe forty-eight hours past five o'clock shadow. It was sexy as hell.

Gloria and I introduced Toryn and Marco and we boarded the train. Gloria and Toryn sat together, playing cards and bickering. They'd become such good friends that they acted like siblings. They seemed to like arguing more than getting along, so I tried not to intervene when my anti-conflict personality reared up.

Marco and I talked and watched the scenery go by. The day was bright, and buildings along the mostly urban route cast strong shadows across the ground. I scanned backyards for children playing, but mostly saw empty dirt lots with the occasional scrawny dog.

I learned a little about Marco's childhood in Vienna, where his mother was a musician and his father a writer. Marco was an only child, and seemed to have enjoyed growing up the way he did. Music had always been a big part of his life. I thought about how parents could provide such amazing advantages to their children when they were willing. Anita did so for Dani, as long as she was able. I hoped the other adults in Dani's life didn't reverse the good.

We arrived at 30th Street Station in the early afternoon. I was eager to see that Dani was doing okay. We'd arranged to meet at the Reading Terminal Market, the historic farmers market in central city. I had some related motives. I wanted to get some Balzac blend coffee at Old City Coffee, and some Oolong at Tea Leaf. We met at the 12th Street Cantina for lunch. Dani found us just as we were being seated and greeted me with a hug. I introduced her to everyone and she looked a little shy, but began recovering quickly.

I was relieved to see her. I didn't see any signs of additional self-harm, but she was pale and her eyes were sunken in shadow. When I asked her, she was clear about her complaints: Chris and Linda were constantly home working their home-based online business; Linda was strange; they were always stressed over the business and money. She'd been thrown into a new school mid-year and didn't know anyone; she missed Boston and her friends. I had the sense that there was more she wasn't telling me.

I asked if she'd heard any updates from Hank.

"He says they're still working on what happened to Brian and whether or not it's connected. Duh." She pushed up the sleeves of her dark green tunic. "I think Dob could have done it, he's so horrible. Or Josephine, for that matter. But I'm not sure why. Having control over my trust, maybe, but it doesn't seem like they really need that. They're greedy though. I'm sure he knew where the family gems were. I called Mom's bank and they said she didn't have a safe deposit box. They made me show them a death certificate before they'd tell me that, if you can believe it."

"I can believe it," Toryn and Gloria

chorused. They were watching Dani intently, as was Marco.

"Is most of her stuff in storage now?" I asked.

"Yeah, I boxed up a little stuff that was important, but I really didn't have time to go through everything. Now here I am, three hundred miles away. Penny, I need to get back to Boston."

The four of us dropped our overnight bags at the B&B, an old brick row house with gleaming wood trim and the requisite high Victorian furniture and floral fabrics. The foyer smelled of lemons. The owners, Marco's friends Lenny and Paul, were out, so we headed out to explore the city a little before dinner, still avoiding the question of three rooms for four of us.

We walked around for a couple of hours looking at shops, historic sites, and people. Gloria found a new-agey store and bought a calming aromatherapy spray and a little crystal "angel of protection" for Dani. I was tempted by a candle that claimed to bring a life of passion, but resisted. I wanted to keep a clear head about Marco and not give in to his easy charm. I didn't need some candle encouraging my libido.

At six, we met up with Lenny and his partner, Paul, who had made reservations for us at an Italian restaurant a few blocks from the B&B. Lenny was a portly middle-aged guy with sparkly blue eyes and very little hair. Paul was tall and thin with a big, off-center nose. He was wearing a gray Henley shirt and jeans complemented by dangly rhinestone earrings and spiky open-toed pumps. His smile was contagious and he hugged each of us. The restaurant was loud, the noise bouncing off the stone and wood interior, but the host showed us to a large table tucked in back and suddenly it felt quite intimate.

We found our places around the big round, Marco to my right, Paul to my left. Marco and Lenny each chose a bottle of wine and ordered for the table. Lenny and Paul asked about our visit, and we took turns telling them about Dani. Gloria, Toryn, and Marco had all become enthusiasts for Dani's welfare.

I had a pretty good idea of where Chris and Linda (and now Dani) lived, and I asked Lenny and Paul about the area and the schools. They said the area was transitional: trying to gentrify, but like many areas of the city, there just wasn't enough cash flow to bring it all the way out of hard times. The recession had been a big setback, of course. The public schools in that district were rough, they said, very rough. I glanced at Marco, who took my hand and held it.

"She's strong, and she looked okay today—maybe a bit tired," he said. "You can learn more over coffee tomorrow." He got up to use the restroom and it struck me as vaguely odd that he took his phone off the table and pocketed it when he went, but he wasn't gone long and I let it go.

The wine came and Marco poured a glass for me. It was light-bodied and red, Italian. Outside of my usual routine, and proof that you miss a lot when stuck in a rut. I liked it a little too much. By the time dinner arrived I'd had two glasses and was very relaxed. The old-world feel of the restaurant, the sounds of people enjoying an evening with friends, and the smell of fresh bread, garlic, and herbs all washed over me. The touch of Marco's leg against mine seemed full of promise, but I was arguing with myself about giving in to the attraction.

Toryn and Paul discussed fishing, while Gloria and Lenny talked about working in service industries. Marco and I found we shared a hobby of spoiling our nieces and made plans to shop sales on Newbury Street when we got back home. His phone vibrated a couple of times on the table, but he discreetly turned it off and gave me his full attention.

Dinner was amazing—I had ravioli stuffed with ricotta, kale, and artichoke hearts. Marco had linguini and clams and we shared. Another glass of wine and I was pretty sure I was falling for him. When he leaned in I could smell that warm balsam soap. I could feel the desire in his eyes and I could almost relax into it. I was nagged by why such a hot guy would take such an interest in me, and I was nagged just a little by thoughts of Will and the still-present sting of the David heartbreak. I told myself the Will thing was just old habit—we didn't stand a chance with such distance between us. The David thing, on the other hand, couldn't be rationalized away. The only option was to try to forget it and hope the pain would eventually pass. It might help to focus on the man sitting next to me. It wasn't so hard to do. I decided that just three rooms at the B&B made a whole lot of sense.

I was a tiny bit wobbly on the way back to the B&B and enjoyed Marco's arm steadying me. I felt like a bit of a fool to have gotten so tipsy, but I was a happy fool.

Back at the B&B Marco pulled me aside into the sitting room and kissed me. Long and slow and full of what I read to be intention. Then he held me to him, my head on his chest, and he whispered, "I had a wonderful time tonight, Penny. I'll see you in the morning." I pulled back and looked at him. He said, "I've arranged to stay with an old friend tonight. I'll have breakfast with her in the morning and meet you at the train station."

His words stung right from my still-tingling mouth down to my gut. I decided not to make matters worse for myself. I would act like it was all perfectly expected—three rooms, after all. He probably had a woman in every city. "Okay. Thanks for tonight. I'll see you tomorrow." I barely managed it. He smiled and turned to Lenny, who was coming into the room to say goodnight.

"Give Marcella my love," Lenny said.

Paul walked us upstairs to our rooms, Gloria and Toryn giving me glances to ask if everything was okay. I was holding back tears, so I just shook my head to fend them off. I could tell them all about what a rat Marco was later.

I collapsed onto the frilly bed and crumpled in on my stupid drunk self. I didn't know how I would manage the train ride home, but I would just have to enlist Gloria and Toryn to insulate me from the playboy. On what planet was it okay to have a date like that and then go stay with another woman? I should have trusted my fears. I only cried a little before falling asleep under the silly romantic canopy.

In the morning I rallied, packed up, thanked Lenny and Paul, and hit the streets. My day's goals were to find out how Dani was really doing and get home without having to deal with Marco. Dani was waiting at the coffee shop she'd picked, and I was glad to see her and refocus on the real reason for my trip to Philly. Unfortunately, I couldn't tear my mind off Marco waking up next to Marcella, who in my imagination had waist-length silken black hair, big gray cat eyes, and perfect curves filling out clothes that were high fashion and effortless. Except no clothes now. Only satin skin, warm against Marco. Lovely Marcella. I shrugged my shoulders to shake the image and focused on Dani.

She still looked tired, but what teenager doesn't at eight o'clock on a Sunday morning?

"Is your school okay?" I asked.

"Not really. I mean, the kids all have their groups and they don't need a new kid. The popular girls snub me, the nerdy girls don't like me, I'm not a jock, and I really don't want to hang with the druggie kids. Last week a guy shoved me against a locker and stuck his tongue practically down my throat and grabbed my crotch. I almost threw up. Now I have to do everything I can to avoid him because, well, he's scary like that."

"How awful! Please tell me you told

someone at school."

"I told my adviser, but Penny, they have a lot bigger things to worry about at that school. There are drugs and weapons and fights all the time. People aren't allowed to wear gang signs, but they just make up new ones, like rolling one sleeve up or untying one shoe. There's no way for the teachers to keep up. A boy groping a girl in the hallway isn't a big deal."

"Has anyone from Family Services here come to visit you or set you up with counseling?"

"No, but it's okay. I don't need it. I just need to know who killed my mom." She'd been avoiding eye contact, but she stole a glance at me when she said this. Then she looked down again, where she was making a design by connecting rings of the wet bottom of her mug on the table.

"Have you heard from Hank and Jenny?" I asked.

"Hank said Uncle Dob is under some sort of investigation—he didn't say what, only that it had to do with business. Maybe that's why he was so stressed out and mean. He said that there aren't any leads on Brian's death. It all sounds pretty useless to me. Nobody is making any progress at all on who killed Mom, and I'm not sure they're really even trying."

"We won't give up, okay? Hey, I stopped by to see Harry. He sends his love."

She smiled a wistful smile.

I continued, "Are you gonna be okay here with Chris and Linda and your school?

I'm worried about you."

"Chris and Linda are lazy, bickering idiots." I was glad to have her alone and have her warmed up and talking, but not happy with what I was hearing. "But I don't want to get them in trouble or anything. I just want to get back home. I'm gonna find a way."

"Does any of this have anything to do with a guy back in Boston?" I asked.

"No. Why would you say that?" Her voice was grumpy and her eyes darted around.

"Condom box in the trash at the apartment. It's okay, I'm not saying there's something wrong with that, but it might be good for you to tell me?"

"It's not really something I can talk about."

"Why not?"

"Because nobody can find out."

"Nobody like who? Why would it be a big problem that you have a boyfriend?"

Her eyes filled with tears. She didn't say anything.

"It's confidential, Dani, we can keep that agreement even if I'm not your counselor anymore."

"He's my voice teacher—Michael." She looked at me with those big eyes, waiting for my reproach. "I really like him. He's smart and talented and he believes in me. When I get back home we're going to take a trip to New York because he wants to introduce me to some people he knows there. Did I ever tell you he went to Juilliard? And got to perform on Broadway once?"

I wasn't sure what to say. Supporting her was the most important thing. "It can't be easy keeping this secret," I finally managed.

She seemed relieved that I was going to be a friend about it and she spilled her story. He was twenty-two, and she'd been seeing him for about six months. Her mom had seen them flirting and had cancelled her lessons, and it was only when she got to Dob's that she could start again, but then Dob cancelled too.

"Have you been in contact with him since you got here?"

"Yeah. We text and stuff. I need to get home so I can see him but even more so I can find out who murdered Mom. Please help me, Penny. I've got to figure this out."

I was out of time. I had to get to the train station. "We'll find answers. Don't do anything without talking to me first, okay? You can call me now, so do."

We said our goodbyes and I gave her Gloria's gifts and hurried out to catch a cab.

Riding along in the cab I thought of a million questions about the voice teacher. A six-year age difference wasn't a big deal, but Dani was only sixteen! He had to know it was unethical to date a student. Was she with him the nights she said she was with friends? What had his reaction been when Anita tried to separate them? Had there been a confrontation? I started to get riled up with worry. Who the hell was this guy? I determined to find out his last name and see what I could learn about him.

Toryn, Gloria, and Marco were waiting on one of the pew-like wooden benches in the station when I rushed in. Our train was boarding and I shuffled my way past Gloria to a window and pulled her in. Marco sat across the aisle and leaned forward to look at me. He hadn't shaved and his scruffy beard was even sexier. Lucky Marcella.

"Penny, this is a long ride. If I've done something to make you mad we should talk."

Gloria must have agreed because she got up and switched places with him. Traitor.

"Is this about last night?"

I burrowed down in my coat so that the collar came up to my nose. I didn't look at him. How could he even talk to me about this? He was fresh out of the shower with *her*, no doubt.

"We don't have to talk about it." I heard the edge in my voice and took a deep breath to calm it. "I'm not looking to have a claim on you." I meant to stop there but I was too angry. "I must have misunderstood about you coming on this trip, about dinner, about that kiss." I wished I would shut up. "I was ready to see what might happen with us, but it was a mistake. Exactly the kind of mistake I try so hard not to—"

"You should know," he interrupted, saving me from myself, "that when I said I was staying with an old friend, I meant it literally. Marcella is a friend of my family. She's eighty."

Huh. I didn't know if I should believe him. He could be totally lying and I wouldn't know. And if it was true, was he such a crappy communicator that he couldn't have clarified that last night? I was silent. Maybe pouty. Just a little.

"I'm sorry I wasn't clear. I guess I thought you assumed I was staying someplace else based on the reservation at the B&B. But I thought about it and while I wanted you to think I was a gentleman, maybe I also wanted to see if you would be jealous. I'm sorry."

I looked out the window. Maybe he was the kind of person who just kept talking when he was nervous or thought you wouldn't like what he said. I kept quiet to see what might be next.

"Will you have dinner with me Friday night? Let me make it up to you? I'll cook. I can, you know."

I didn't answer, just kept looking out the window at the inside of the train station as we pulled out.

"Okay. You have to think about it. I picked up an Uno deck. Will you play me while you think?"

We played cards for a long time, talking a little. I wasn't sure what to do about the dinner invitation. Maybe this was a good time to end things, before I got in any deeper. I'd made a mistake by dating him at all. I didn't have the energy to get all emotionally involved with someone.

It was raining in Boston when we got home, and we were all a little crabby from being cooped up too long. Marco gave me a tentative peck goodbye and headed home.

I took a deep breath, and resolved to let the rain be my tears and this the end of dating Marco.

Gloria and I said goodbye to Toryn and I

turned to walk away. Out of the corner of my eye I saw Toryn slip her some cash.

"You are not sly!" I said, spinning back. "Gloria, you bet against me?"

"No." Gloria feigned innocence. "I bet in favor of your virtue."

Some people could play that off as a compliment, but not Gloria. This is the woman who once said "Look what virginity got Mary! She still got pregnant and she had more than your average parenting challenge with that one." No, Gloria had no place for chastity, virtue, or even restraint.

Toryn beamed with the reversal of his defeat, and I stomped and scuffed my shit-kickers all the way home.

CHAPTER TWELVE

On Monday I called DCF to find out if they had worked with Family Services in Philly to arrange a home visit. They said they had made the request and were waiting.

I called Hank and Jenny. Jenny answered. I told her about my visit to Dani and my concerns. I had promised Dani confidentiality so I couldn't tell Jenny my worries about Michael the musical letch. How was I going to get a name for him?

"She called here," Jenny said. "I'm worried about her in that school, and Chris isn't a competent parent, especially not for a girl in a crisis."

"Jenny, would it give you any leverage if I wrote a letter recommending her return to Boston and her school?"

"It might. I think Chris was teetering on the edge of letting us keep her here, but he feels like he would look bad giving up his own daughter. Frankly, I think he would be relieved. An official recommendation might be just the excuse he needs to make the right decision."

"I'd rather not work through DCF if possible, just to avoid complications." I was thinking of what would happen if Vivian found out. "Do you think it would work if I sent a letter directly to him on letterhead?"

"It's worth a try."

Dani called that evening. "Penny, hey, um, I sent you some stuff in an email. Did you see it yet?"

"No, Dani, what did you send?" I didn't like the sound of her voice. She was shaky.

"My dad, well, he's a musician, you know, kind of. And I found some of his files and I was just listening to hear his stuff and some of it was a little weird, you know, I mean, I think it was about my mom and I'm just really sad and freaked out."

"Tell me more. I'm sorry I didn't see the email."

"When nobody was home I was looking through some stuff in Dad and Linda's office. He keeps his music stuff in there too and I wanted to see if he was working on new stuff still or what." She paused and I switched my phone to speaker and put it down so I could crank up my old laptop. "I found a big fat file that had a bunch of CDs and some pictures. It even had Mom's flight itinerary from when she went to India. There were pictures of her—I guess they were from when they were married." She sounded a little embarrassed so I didn't press.

Dani continued, "My dad's okay—I mean he's messed up and stuff, but not evil or anything. I guess he just really loved her. Do you think they broke up because Mom was having an affair or something?"

Dani's dad wasn't in Philly when Anita died. He said he was in the Poconos, but did we have proof? He was in Boston around the time Brian was hit, but I didn't know exactly when he'd arrived. If he was obsessed with Anita and jealous of Brian, the two murders made perfect sense.

"I hear you, Dani, but your mom would give your dad her flight itinerary when she went on an international trip like that. And while the rest of the stuff is upsetting, of course, it doesn't seem extraordinary that he has some mementos of their marriage."

I opened up my email but decided to wait until I got off the phone to access the files. "Is anything else going on there? School and stuff?"

"School's the same. I talked to Hank. It turns out that business trouble Dob's in is a federal investigation for laundering money! No wonder those two are so freaky and on edge all the time. Something to do with their business, but Dob says he didn't know anything. He says it wasn't his fault, but some guy who buys stuff from him. I think he's lying, because he was so paranoid."

"That's a lot going on. I don't have nearly as much news to share, but I did talk with Jenny and I know she really wants to bring you here."

"What if I start getting in a lot of trouble here? Then maybe Dad won't want me. I could get caught with drugs, break my curfew, bring nasty boys home—that kind of thing."

"You've thought this through," I said. "But no, I think that might be more of a last resort, okay? Let's try to keep you clean. What if your testimony is needed when we find your mom's killer? Do you want them to write you off as a druggie teen?" I thought it was pretty quick thinking on my part. The last thing we needed was Dani going down the wrong road even if it was for a good reason. I'd seen plenty of my friends travel the wrong path for rebellion, to experiment, to piss off their parents, and they'd found it hard to find their way back. "Promise me. Give Jenny a chance to try again with your dad, and talk with me before you try anything like that, okay?"

When Dani and I hung up I opened the audio files she'd sent. There were two. "Nine Planet Love Song" was melodic but awkward.

"Stolen Rubies" was heavy-metal harsh. The refrain caught my attention. It went: "*Untraceable, I see you lace and all, stolen from under me, I build your effigy.*" Sure, it was lyrically troublesome, and it was creepy too.

Will called, saving me from my wild imagination. I could interpret any piece of information as danger for Dani. Will and I caught up on work and our families. I told him what was happening with Dani, and about my trip to Philly (leaving Marco out). We bantered. We could talk and laugh and tease each other until the end of time. I loved the resonance of his voice and the careful way he reminded me of my quirks when he formed a joke. When my memory failed he'd bring up food, a sure-fire way to access whatever part of my brain was hiding something. "Remember?" he might say. "It was on the river, and we saw the barges pass... Okay, remember the thick pan-sautéed noodles with the peanut sauce and vegetables?"

"Oh!" I'd say. "The place with the really long bar, and zinnias on the table." Food memory, that's what I had. Ask me about a city, I'll tell you what I ate.

I thought of Marco. I was starting to have some serious food memories with Marco. Will loved food, but he was summer corn, garden greens, and crock pot stew, whereas Marco was Roquefort and apricots with French Syrah.

Will and I signed off late with sighing and promises to talk again soon. By that time I was curled under my Grandma Pottery Barn quilt, ready for sleep.

I was jolted awake the next morning by my phone. Owen. My mind jumped to all the bad places.

"Aunt Helen died. Mrs. Kaminsky found her when she went to check in last night. She called me late."

Aunt Helen was my mom's sister. She lived in our childhood home, having moved in with Mom after Dad died. When Mom died, she stayed. She didn't have children of her own, but she had a strong community in Carmel, including a lot of neighbors who helped look out for her. She was old, but this was unexpected. She'd been self-sufficient, if not as feisty as she once was.

Aunt Helen was the end of the line of our elders, leaving me and Owen with a clear view of death's door.

"Oh," was my whole reply. Then

eventually, "I guess we have to go there, huh?"

"I guess so," Owen said.

Owen looked at flights while we were on the phone. He decided to drive down the next day and stay with me. Then we'd catch an early flight to Indianapolis, rent a car, and go "home." I needed to take some time off work because there were more than a few details to manage when we got there. It was the house: the whole damn, solid-packed, waste nothing, throw-nothing-away house. It held everything three adults and two children could store from 1975 until now. I wondered if we could just burn it down. Not to collect insurance—I'm not a criminal—just to get rid of it and sell the lot.

I hit Vivian's office first thing when I got to work.

"The policy is really about immediate family." Her voice sounded tight and crisp. "I'm not going to stop you from going, but I will ask you to minimize your time out of the office."

"I'm really sorry," I said. She must be thinking this would be a good time to replace me.

"These things happen. Do what you have to do," she said.

I found myself crossing my arms in front of me at the empty sound of her words. I wondered if there weren't a few phrases we'd all said too many times. No way to make them sound fresh.

Gloria and Owen were popping popcorn

and watching reruns of *3rd Rock from the Sun* when I got home Wednesday evening. "Buncha fogies, I see," I said as I hugged Owen.

We were all tired so we ordered Chinese and talked through more reruns of *3rd Rock*. Owen updated us on the girls and Maria, and we told him about our jobs and the ongoing search for Anita's killer. Given that I hadn't wanted to discuss work when we talked last, there was a lot to tell. Gloria included Marco in the Philly-trip story, and so there were prying questions from my nosy little brother.

I was probably a little snappish, the creeping stomachache already coming along in anticipation of going back to *the house*. We decided to put off our Carmel strategy for the plane ride. We would have to play most of it by ear anyway.

CHAPTER THIRTEEN

We were at our childhood home by noon on Thursday. Our energy was high, maybe manic. We had big plans to knock out everything in less than two days and head home. Our cousin Bill, my mom's brother's son, was doing the funeral arrangements, so our main job was the house.

We parked the rental car in the driveway and looked at the brown winter lawn, the dead hydrangea flowers along the flagstone walk, and the freshly painted gray siding. I tried to view the place with fresh eyes, as though it wasn't the driveway where I'd learned to roller-skate and ride a bike. Not the lawn where I built snowmen. Not the dogwood tree I climbed. Because if I thought about those things, I'd also think about how Mom couldn't tolerate the sound of us playing and would send us out to the yard so much that it became a punishment. Or I'd relive the time when I was sixteen and had to sleep in my car on a cold night because my parents locked me out for being six minutes late for my curfew. I pushed the memories out and focused on forward motion.

We went around to the back door, through the entryway we'd used as a mudroom, always piling coats and boots and backpacks on the floor and blocking the door. I remembered spilling in after school, starving. I could usually find individually wrapped American cheese slices in the fridge. I'd peel the slick cheese from its wrapper in perfectly geometrical shapes and match them with crackers or apple slices.

The kitchen smelled the same, stale, like long-damp wood, with a hint of bleach. The faded yellow-flowered linoleum floors were spotless, the Formica countertop too. There were some family photos magneted to the fridge, mostly pictures of Owen's girls and Bill's son.

Through the door to our right was the formal dining room, not large but sufficient for when we had the extended family over when we were kids. There was a rectangular shiny-wood dinette set, a sideboard against the outer wall to the right, and a big picture window to the front yard. In the traditional central-foyer tradition, the living room was across the entryway, and the stairs in the middle.

We went upstairs and surveyed the job. We knew the bedroom closets were jam-packed, that there would be stuff under the beds and stuffed in dresser drawers. I closed the door to Sarah's old room without going in. Owen pulled down the stairs to the attic, climbed up, and reported boxes and small pieces of old furniture. I envisioned getting one of those construction chutes and sliding everything out the little attic window into a dumpster.

We descended, but not so far as to the basement. I was terrified of the basement as a child and now again, but for different reasons. There would be countless hours of digging and sorting through musty boxes. The basement was not reliably dry, so we could count on our ghosts being mildewed.

We landed at the kitchen table after Owen put water on for tea. We looked at each other for a long time. I picked at my fingernails to the point he finally got irritated and kicked me under the table. Then he got up and dialed a number from memory. Pizza. I had hopes that it would help.

We decided to knock out a closet while we waited. I took trash bags from under the kitchen sink and we went to the front hall. Easy. Hats, boots, coats, scarves, umbrellas, and random junk. We made a bag for Goodwill and one for trash. We were flying high and went for a cabinet full of board games and stuff in the living room. Most of that went into the trash—nobody needed Sorry with missing pieces. I tried to pitch stuff quickly, but the Trouble game got me. I remembered sitting on the floor with Trouble on the coffee table, playing with Sarah. Mom came in and snapped at us because the dice popper was too loud and it was disturbing her as she sat at the kitchen table watching *General Hospital* on her little TV. It must have been a school holiday, or Sarah and I were both home sick. Sarah was home sick a lot.

The doorbell rang and saved me from myself. Nothing stuffs feelings like a deep pan pizza.

While we were eating a text chimed in.
Marco: Hiya.
Everything OK?

I hadn't called or texted about my trip,
so figured I should explain. I'd forgotten why I
was so mad at him anyway.

Me: Hey. Yeah. Sorta.
My aunt died
my brother and I flew home
be back Sunday
Marco: So sorry!
Call if you want to talk.
Can I pick you up from BOS?

I'd hesitated a while, but ultimately
decided it wouldn't hurt to have him pick us
up. After our early dinner we returned to
cleaning. I felt like I was suffocating on dust,
boxing up china and tchotchkes in the dining
room. The doorbell rang again. Owen opened
the front door for Mrs. Kaminsky, who was red
with tears. She hugged Owen and looked at
me heaving stuff into trash bags. I rose to
greet her but intercepted a laser glare. Either
I did something wrong a long time ago, or she
thought my cleaning methods were
disrespectful. I shook her hand and apologized
for being dusty. She was brittle.

"Helen was a dear, dear friend,
children," she sobbed. "I'm beside myself
about all this."

With who-shall-show-sympathy-for-
whom clearly established, Owen and I both
launched in and did our best.

"Come have some tea, won't you?"
Owen affected just a little bit of Brit, surely a
mistake influenced by the falseness of his

warmth. I stifled a giggle.

Owen led Mrs. Kaminsky to the kitchen, which was only partially dismantled. I closed cabinets and tried to restore order. Owen put on the kettle. "This house has seen so much death," Mrs. Kaminsky said. Was her tone accusatory? Had we cursed her with our family tragedies so close to her perfect home? "First little Sarah, then your father, then your mother, now Helen."

"We won't quote you on the real estate listing," Owen teased.

Mrs. Kaminsky frowned. We'd lost track of the object of the game: to console her. I leapt in.

"I'm sure some young family will bring joy back here soon, Mrs. Kaminsky. You have been such a rock to our family through the years. Someone will be lucky to have you for a neighbor."

Owen got into the groove. "It must have been awful finding Aunt Helen like you did. I'm so sorry it happened that way. Are you doing okay? Sleeping and all? Have your kids been here to see you?"

"Oh yes." She was starting to look pleased, but taking pains to hide it. "Pippa and the kids were here yesterday. Such a great joy to me, always." She took a cup of tea from Owen. "I've spoken to Bill about the arrangements for Helen. I think you'll be pleased. I know Helen will."

"Thank you, Mrs. Kaminsky," I said. "It means a lot to have your guidance on these things. You were very special to Aunt Helen."

"And Bill is very grateful for your help,"

Owen added. It was safe to assume that was a lie.

"I remember when you were all small," she said. "Sarah was still in diapers when we moved in. Your mother was overwhelmed, but my kids were already in school, so I would come and bounce Sarah on my knee while your mother did housework."

"Excuse me, I'm so sorry," I stammered. "My stomach is a little upset from the pizza, I've got to—" I hurried upstairs. Away from that woman, away from the vision of Sarah in diapers, often on my hip as our mother cooked. Sarah, tiny and fair and happy. Sarah singing, always singing. From the time she was in diapers, she sang songs only she could understand.

Sarah was insulated from our parents, or so I liked to think. Owen and I fed her and changed her and played with her. We did everything we could to keep her happy. I committed myself to giving her all the things I wanted from Mom. All the things I never got. I responded when she called out or cried, I let her make a mess with her toys, I let her get muddy and play with the neighbor's dogs, and sometimes I let her be the boss, knowing what it felt like to be ignored and powerless all the time.

In the upstairs bathroom I splashed my face with water. I sat on the toilet lid and concentrated on breathing. In, out. I don't know how long I was there, but I stood up when I heard the front door close. Owen was on his way up the stairs. I met him in the hallway and we went back down without speaking. He was moving more slowly than before. We took up our chores in silence.

We both jumped when my phone chimed with a text.

Dani: I want to come home to Boston!
My dad is drinking again.
Me: Do you feel unsafe?
Dani: No, just unhappy I guess
Me: Call me or police if you feel unsafe
And call if you just need to talk
Dani: Can't talk now
Will call soon
Me:Take care of yourself
I'm here if you need me

A chill went through me thinking about Dani in the dirty home of a father she hardly knew, and now he was drunk? I needed to get her out of there. I was ready to get on a plane to Philly and remove her myself, but I knew that what I thought was right and what the system would allow were not the same thing.

I was still stewing over Dani (and complaining nonstop to Owen about the situation) when we finally gave up cleaning around midnight. We'd stuck with mostly safe stuff: folding and bagging clothes for Goodwill, boxing kitchenware, boxing books. I was careful not to look at book titles. If there was anything valuable in the mix it would be good luck for the library, because I wasn't going to get carried away by the tide of memory from when I read *The Thornbirds* or the first time I read *Gone with the Wind*.

At the top of the stairs Owen and I paused, suitcases in hand. My room had been turned into a guest room, and then became Aunt Helen's room. Sarah's room hadn't really changed, and the door wasn't going to open before it had to.

Owen tilted his head in the direction of his room and we both went in there. He would sleep on the top bunk, like he had as a kid, and I would sleep below, where he'd always piled his junk. The room looked odd with its blue sports-themed bedspreads neatly tucked in, his trophies still on a high shelf, Hardy Boys mysteries neatly ordered on his bookshelf. I thought of the Nancy Drew series neatly shelved in Sarah's room. So many ghosts.

I changed and brushed my teeth. My eyes looked hollow and my faint freckles stood out against my pale face. I wondered where all my blood had gone. I jumped when I saw a reflection of something moving behind me, but it was just the lights of a car turning into the drive next door.

I climbed into the narrow hard bed and listened to Owen trying to get comfortable up above.

"Owen, do you ever feel like maybe life's all prearranged—like the template has been laid and it's just waiting for the spray paint?"

"No, Penny. You're not going to move into this house, grow old, and die here with a basement full of crap."

We were silent. The creak of the bunk bed reminded me of the noises of the house when I was a child: the bathroom door opening and closing as Sarah and Owen got ready for bed, Mom and Dad fighting. Sarah singing, and in later years crying herself to sleep.

I launched out of bed and ran to the bathroom, where I reduced the calorie load of the pizza. It had felt like a cement piling in my stomach anyway. Over the next hours I repeated the performance until it was only dry heaves, but I couldn't rest, couldn't settle my stomach or my body enough to stay in bed. Owen climbed down and put a practiced hand on my forehead.

"Kinda clammy from puking, but no fever," he diagnosed.

"You're a good daddy," I said. He sat on the lower bunk with me and I cried for a long time. When I took my face out of the pillow and looked at him I saw that he was crying too, quiet grown-up tears.

When I was thoroughly exhausted I lay down and Owen tucked me in before climbing back to his bunk.

We slept blessedly late—8:30, which must have seemed to Owen like sleeping half the day away. I was weak and hungry. We decided to get out of the house. We went to the local pancake house and stuffed ourselves, then bought industrial trash bags and went back to the house. I'd left my phone there, and when I checked it I saw a missed call from Dani. I tried to call her back, but didn't get an answer.

Mid-morning, cousin Bill called to invite us over for dinner with him and his wife. There was no way to say no.

We worked fast and hard and seemed to make absolutely no impact on the job. I tried to use my arm as an excuse—I mean it definitely made things harder—but I'd made the mistake of telling Owen that it wasn't a really bad break and he was using that against me. He twice rejected my suggestion to burn the sucker down. When I'd thought of every possible solution to getting out of the job, and found none of them workable, I tried them all again in my mind with the same conclusion.

"I'm going up," I said, standing. Owen looked up, then got up and followed me.

I opened the door and walked into Sarah's room. Lavender, yellow, and pink. Her My Pretty Pony collection was lined up on her bookcase above the Nancy Drew series. Her bed was neatly made with its lacy lavender spread, stuffed animals arranged against her pillow. I powered in and began opening drawers. Most of her stuff was cleaned out. The closet held only a few favorite dresses, but everything else was gone. I hoped someone had given it to charity, rather than "handing it down" to some child who knew it was from the little girl who died. I took one of the ponies—the lavender one I remembered as her favorite—and went into Owen's room and put it in my bag. Owen took the other ponies, one for each girl, and we quickly bagged everything else and got out.

Bill's house was a short drive away, a newer two-story home with triangular peaks across the front and a brick façade betrayed by vinyl siding the rest of the way around. Bill and his wife Dee Dee were both overweight with thinning hair and deep frown lines. They welcomed us warmly and asked how the house was coming. They updated us on the funeral plans and we laughed about old Mrs. Kaminsky and her helpful suggestions.

We drank gin and tonics before dinner, wine with dinner, and Bill and Dee Dee moved on to Jack Daniel's after dinner. Bill and Dee Dee bickered over details of the funeral services—who had done the most phone calls, and what still needed to be done. The tension felt all too familiar, and I imagined them in a full-blown fight later. I wanted to get out of there before my tummy turned on me again, so I pretended to stifle a yawn and looked at Owen.

"Bill and Dee Dee, you guys were so nice to have us over and feed us great food," I said. "It's really great to see you both looking so well and all settled into your new house. It's a great house."

"Yeah, it's been too long between visits." Owen stood as he spoke, and I stood too. "I guess we'll see you tomorrow. Will you let us know how we can help with the service?"

Soon we were out, never more grateful to be in a rental car. I tried Dani again, but still no answer.

Saturday was basement day. Oh, dreaded day of must (note double meaning). We opened the one high little basement window we could pry open, and welcomed the dribble of cold fresh air as we began sorting. We had convinced each other it would be easier than we thought and made a pact to get it finished before the funeral.

By lunchtime we were sneezing and coated in dirt and dust, but overall unharmed. We went out for sub sandwiches, then back to the dungeon. We did okay until Owen found Dad's old military uniform, with the pins still attached.

"Odd to think that dad was smaller than I am," Owen said.

"He always seemed so big." I had nothing insightful to say. I was mentally scrambling about how to support my baby brother, who had seen me through our first night as if he were my big brother.

"He never talked about it," Owen said. "But I remember him crying over old war movies."

"I do too. Mom would yell at him if he tried to watch them, but he did anyway and he cried and he and Mom fought about it."

It seemed like my dad had been permanently damaged by the war. He didn't engage in life much—he worked, drank, and worked more. Mom was understandably depressed—a suburban housewife married to a damaged man. She drank too much too. I'd often wondered how they got together, but they weren't the types to tell stories about their courtship.

"I guess we had training when it comes to avoiding the past." Owen and I had often commented on how other people seemed to remember so much more of their childhoods than we did. We both had some very clear memories, but maybe a dozen or so for the whole of our childhoods.

"Look where hiding from their past landed them, Owen: alcoholism and depression. I don't want to go there."

"No," he said, almost wistfully.

When we were too tired to do any more, I took a break with a glass of Aunt Helen's sherry and sat down with a pen and paper.

The funeral was at four o'clock, by which time Owen and I had finished the basement. We showered and dressed in our churchiest clothes and showed up at the church where our mother used to drag us on those Sundays when she felt the call to see and be seen with her children. It was the church where we had the service for Sarah, then for Dad, then Mom. But Aunt Helen's funeral was the first time I took the podium.

"Aunt Helen was the last of her generation in our family," I started, then I looked out at the church full of people and froze. Public speaking was a big, big fear of mine. I looked at Owen. He smiled, and I took the encouragement. "But I didn't know her as well as my brother did," I improvised quickly. I checked the floor for tripping hazards and crossed to the steps to make my escape.

Owen mounted the four steps before I could descend them. He put one hand on my arm and the other on my back and guided me back to the podium. I itched from my throat to my, uh, derriere. I put my notes back on the podium and lowered my head to within about a foot of them. I read.

"She was my mother's sister, one of

three children raised on a farm here in Indiana. Aunt Helen went to college, which was much more unusual for a woman back then. She studied Library Science. Many of you remember her years at the Carmel Library." I was shifting from foot to foot behind the podium and Owen was still at my side, an insistent presence. I kept my head down and read. "Aunt Helen was around a lot when we were growing up. She babysat when my parents went out, she ate dinner with us, and always loved a good board game. Our baby sister, Sarah, was her special favorite, but then Sarah was the special favorite to all of us."

That was it. Limit. Human capacity. I turned to Owen in a full-body plea to release me.

Owen guided me to his side as he stepped to the podium and read my notes. "Aunt Helen used to bring us children's music on cassette tapes from the library, and Sarah would play them over and over until she could sing every song. After Sarah died, Aunt Helen put her own grief aside and came and stayed with us and took care of my brother, Owen, and me. Years later, after our father died, and we were both grown and gone from the house, Aunt Helen moved back in to help take care of Mom. It was wonderful knowing that Mom had her sister there with her. The two of them grew old together. When Mom died a few years ago, Aunt Helen took it hard, but she was always resilient. She mourned and then got right back into life, returning to her bridge club and her garden club and volunteering at the library. We'll miss her. I hope we learned a lot from her because she was a strong, kind, and giving woman who never gave up. I think she died happy—independent and busy until the end."

Owen held me and guided me back to our seats.

After the graveside service, we returned to the church basement for the feast the church ladies prepared. I wondered what the world will do without church ladies, because I felt fairly certain they weren't making them anymore. We ate chicken salad on white bread, vegetable sticks with ranch dip, and cookies. We drank coffee that tasted like the big brown plastic dispenser. We chatted. As soon as we were able, we left.

"Tell me about Sarah," I said in the car. I needed to have the unspeakable spoken.

"Sarah was a ginger, curly and buoyant. Sarah sang. She laughed. Sarah almost never cried until she couldn't dance, and then she cried. She had surgery on her heart. Again and again. She got weak. Sarah understood that they couldn't fix her heart and she cried because she wanted to dance and because she wanted to grow up and she knew she couldn't. Sarah died when she was seven and we were never the same."

We handed the house keys to the real estate agent with little ceremony and no regret. My last look back at the house brought a sigh of relief, second only to how I imagined feeling if we'd burned the sucker down.

Marco picked us up at the airport and

took us to my place. It had snowed nearly a foot while we were gone and the city looked innocent and lovely. Owen kissed me goodbye and started his drive home laden with toys we'd bought in the airport for the girls.

"You look worn out," Marco said. "How about if I pick up something for dinner, feed you, then let you rest."

"That sounds great. Thanks." I just wanted a hot shower and some dreamless sleep.

Marco ran out and returned with fresh ravioli, sauce, and bread from the Italian market. He poured a glass of wine for me then made himself at home in the kitchen. He made enough for Gloria, although we didn't know when she would be getting home. Gloria must have had a date or something, so it was just the two of us.

When he asked me if I wanted to talk about it I said yes. And I did, a little. I told him the story of the trip and a little about my childhood: Sarah, my parents, how Owen and I stuck together. I didn't go into a lot of detail because, well, I didn't do much detail when it came to the past. I showed him Sarah's pony.

Part of me thought it might be good to say more—like maybe I could move on with more clarity once I put everything on the table. If Marco knew how much my childhood had messed me up, if *I* acknowledged it better, maybe it could be more manageable. Maybe it wouldn't sneak up and bite me in my most vulnerable moments. But I couldn't wade back in. The past few days had been more than I could handle and I wanted to get back to my grown-up life. I wanted to think about the future.

We sat with our wine in the darkening living room, and I noticed that he didn't reach for the lights. When I stepped away to go to the bathroom he picked up Gloria's guitar and played. When I came out of the bathroom I froze in place just outside the bathroom door. I leaned against the hallway wall and closed my eyes to listen. Love, sadness, loss, passion, longing, joy, all distilled, cleaned of drama and pretense and given sound. They tangled and untangled from one another. I didn't move. I didn't want him to stop. If I could take my emotions and send them through my fingers into the air maybe they wouldn't come out through my mouth, through my tears. As I listened I learned something about Marco. He felt intensely and he had access to those feelings. Allowing strong emotions into the light isn't easy for most of us and I didn't think it was easy for him, but he'd found his way.

I didn't want a reason to love him.

He put down the guitar, picked up his phone, and hit the button. Was he looking at the clock? Looking for a text? Then he got up and turned to find me leaning there watching him. He shoved his phone into his pocket and smiled his most charming smile.

"There you are," he said. "You need to get some rest. I'll let you get to bed and check on you tomorrow, okay?"

He gave me a kiss on the cheek and turned to leave. I stood frozen against the wall with a flush of regret.

"Marco?"

My voice quavered. He turned back and in four steps he was there, pressing my body hard against the wall, his mouth on mine. I ceded to the force of him. He tugged my hair aside and kissed my neck. The willfulness and adrenaline that had kept me standing the past few days evaporated and I went weak. He slid one arm behind the small of my back, scooped me up, and carried me to bed, his mouth never leaving my skin.

CHAPTER FOURTEEN

The next morning I found a text from Dani.

Dani: Call me

I did.

"Penny, I'm *here*!" she squealed.

"Where?"

"In Boston! Well, Wayland anyway. Somehow Hank and Jenny convinced my dad to let me come stay with them!"

Did my letter work? I guessed she didn't know about that and I decided not to tell her. "Dani, I'm so happy! Are you back at your school?"

"I will be tomorrow! It's great, Penny, and Niles and Leena are paying for me to go back to my voice lessons! Isn't that so nice of them?"

I wanted to do a happy dance because she was finally in a good home, but my joy was ruined by Michael. I didn't want to betray Dani's trust but I wanted to alert Hank and Jenny.

"Dani, maybe you should tell Hank and Jenny about Michael."

"Why?"

"Well, because they're kind of like parents to you and at your age parents would usually know who you're dating."

"No. And you promised not to tell."

On Thursday everyone left work early to stand in line for toilet paper and bread. The forecast called for a blizzard, a nor'easter of epic proportions. I'd been in Boston long enough to learn that my Midwestern sturdiness didn't begin to compare with the hardy New Englanders'. Seriously. If they were going to swarm the supermarkets and convenience stores, I was going to see what was in their baskets and follow suit.

I arrived home with toilet paper, batteries, potato flakes, bread, *People* magazine, cat food, a pair of pliers, and a can of Spam. I wasn't sure why anyone would need cat food *and* Spam, and I didn't know what *People* magazine was good for, but I was going on faith that the other shoppers knew what they were doing.

The snow started in the late afternoon: big wet flakes at first, but as the temperature dropped they got smaller and blew in the rising wind. Gloria and I hunkered down with movies, beer, and popcorn.

I was enjoying the enforced break from everything.

Then Dani called. "I'm at Dob and Jo's. I still have a key so I came after school to find Mom's gems. They must have gotten stuck somewhere because they still aren't back."

My heart jumped. "Dani, it's snowing like hell. What are you doing?"

I looked out the window. There was already at least six inches of fresh snow on top of the twelve from the last storm.

"That's the part I'm not sure about. But I found them! I found a whole box of Mom's family gems and some of the stuff she made too!"

"How did you know where it was?"

"I searched until I found it. I just knew it had to be Dob because, well, I didn't have any better ideas."

"Okay, but can you stay there?"

"No! I'm sure they're trying to come back before it gets worse, but they already shut down the T and I can't get a cab and I'm not really sure what to do."

"Okay. Stay as long as you can. Watch out the window. If you see them coming, get a blanket, wrap it around you, get out whatever door you can and meet me at the bathrooms by the monument. But stay there if you can. It's super cold out."

"Okay…" She sounded scared.

"I'll call you when I'm close."

Gloria was listening to the whole conversation, gesturing and objecting the whole time. But she knew I wouldn't listen.

I put long underwear under my pants, three shirts, two pairs of socks, my shit-stomping boots, jacket, gloves, and hat. At that point I'd lost a good degree of mobility and I was sweating like crazy, but I still had to load my pockets with New England provisions. I grabbed the Spam, some toilet paper, batteries, pliers, matches, and two packets of hot cocoa mix. Gloria frowned and gave me a little bottle of peppermint essential oil.

I hit the snowy streets heavy with

supplies. I hiked a few blocks, the deep snow falling into my boots, and stopped to rearrange because the can of Spam was clanking on the pliers and the batteries were jangling with the peppermint oil. I thought maybe I should keep the book of matches separate from the batteries. I did my best— with half an arm in a cast no less—to rearrange everything and hiked on. It was a little over three miles to Bunker Hill from South Boston, maybe an hour and fifteen on a normal day. Walking was hard. The wind sprayed me with snow and pushed against my progress. I took to the streets to avoid having to climb over the plow piles. There were only a couple of cars when I started, and even though I was tromping through central parts of Boston, the streets emptied as the storm continued to pick up.

It was cold. Beyond cold. My weather app said eleven with a wind chill of six below. My feet were wet and my toes were numb. When the wind gusted it was hard to see where I was going. I argued with myself nonstop. I should stop and rest. I should call someone (what would they do?). I should find some use for the pliers.

I picked up the Freedom Trail for a little while near Faneuil Hall, but then cut across the North End and picked it up again just before the Charlestown Bridge. It had taken me almost two hours to get that far. I had trouble finding the Charlestown Bridge because I got disoriented in the snow-covered streets with visibility next to nothing. I hadn't seen a single person for nearly an hour.

I found the bridge and made my way slowly across. The wind up there was formidable but I kept my head down and my determination up. On the far side of the bridge I finally decided to rest. I needed to gather strength. I sat down at the edge of Paul Revere Park and rested my head on my knees. After a while I found I hadn't regained energy. I was more tired than before.

I looked around. It was a total whiteout. I couldn't see the street from where I sat. I decided I would get up soon and keep going. But first I needed just a catnap. I was so, so sleepy.

I was starting to have those half-asleep funny dream thoughts. A man of authority rushed into a banquet room and dove under a huge round table. He emerged carrying a gigantic sheep. He set the sheep down and turned to me. He shook one long finger in my face and told me I had to go choose a wig.

My phone startled me awake. I grabbed the Spam, the cocoa packets, and finally my phone.

"Hell…" Damn, I was weak.

"Penny, are you okay, are you coming?"

"I am." I closed my eyes.

Dani's voice was insistent. "Penny, where are you? I'm scared here. I need to leave."

I sat up a little. "Huh? Are you at the apartment?"

"No! I'm at Dob and Jo's townhouse. What's wrong? You don't sound right."

"Oh, it's just cold is all. I have batteries."

"Penny, please come here before Dob gets back and finds me with Mom's stuff."

Anita's stuff. Dani. I started to remember. It didn't seem that important though, and I rested my head again.

"Penny!" I heard Dani again. Why did I keep hearing her? "Come to Dob's now. Are you walking? If you aren't walking I'll call the police."

I stood. "No, Dani. Don't call them. I'm walking."

The wind let up long enough for me to get my bearings and I dragged my feet through the ever deepening snow. "I'll be there soon."

I hung up and pocketed the phone, noting "Spam pocket."

Once I was up and moving I revived a little. I was probably less than a mile from the townhouse.

CHAPTER FIFTEEN

Dani was still at Dob's when I arrived. Nobody was moving around in this snow. Well, nobody smart.

Dani had packed her mom's stuff in a backpack and had blankets for each of us. I tried not to think about what was ahead, because I was so cold and wet that part of me just wanted to stay at Dob's come what may. But I needed to get Dani out of there, so we set out into the storm.

It was getting dark and the storm was heavier than ever. Dani was shivering hard.

I tried to distract us.

"Do Hank and Jenny know where you are?"

"I told them I was staying with my friend Kennedy because the storm hit so fast that I couldn't get home from school."

"Have you talked to them? They're probably worried."

"I texted. I said I was okay."

The conversation didn't help us move any faster or feel any warmer. We hadn't even made it off Monument Hill.

"Dani, I think we should find a place to stop."

"The Dodges live a couple of streets

over. I babysit for them. I thought about them earlier but I didn't know what I would tell them. Maybe I just should have gone there instead of dragging you all the way here. I'm really sorry."

Dani had her blanket over her head like a hood and was clutching it around her tightly, still shivering and starting to cry.

"Let's go. I'll handle it," I said.

Two blocks felt like a long walk in the deep and drifting snow, especially since I'd been out in it for hours already. Some spots were thigh-high and the snow soaked our legs and fell into our boots.

We couldn't see the steps leading up to the Dodges' door, so we felt our way up and Dani rang the bell.

A man in his mid-thirties opened the door and looked at us with surprise. He looked a little like Woody Allen.

"Dani," he said, "is everything okay? I mean, well, it must not be! Please come in."

We kicked the snow off of ourselves as well as we could and entered the townhouse.

"Mr. Dodge, this is my friend Penny Wade." Dani paused.

A woman came into the hall with a baby on her hip.

"Dani! What were you doing out in this?"

"Um, well, you know my mom died and stuff, and um, I was staying with Uncle Dob, you know, and I really didn't like it there and I was staying someplace else, but today I went back to get some stuff and then the storm came and I was, uh, locked out, so I called

Penny and she walked all the way from Southie and I waited in the garage. But we couldn't walk all the way back. So I thought maybe you would let us wait here until it clears up a little?"

Mr. and Mrs. Dodge looked at me. I was staring at the baby. Mrs. Dodge clutched her a little tighter.

I glanced at the hall mirror and understood her concern. I had an old blanket over my shoulders, my hat was completely covered in snow, and my coat was bulging with all my heavy supplies. Pale face, stringy hair, and I just dragged a teenager out in dangerous weather.

"I'm so sorry to put you in this position," I said. "I thought I could get her home to my place, but it's just too cold and too hard to walk. The snow is getting really deep."

They smiled politely. Mrs. Dodge said to Dani, "It's dangerous out there. You should know better."

I knew that comment was meant for me.

"But it's good that you're here now. Take off your wet things and come get warm."

Dani and I began dismantling ourselves. We tried not to make a big mess on the entryway floor but there was snow everywhere and it was turning to puddles. I tried to wipe up with my hat and gloves but they were soaked. The Dodges watched us indulgently for a minute, then Mr. Dodge went off to get some towels.

"Let me put your things in the dryer,"

Mrs. Dodge said.

Dani wadded her hat, gloves, and coat in her blanket and handed the bundle to Mrs. Dodge, who turned her attention to me. I gave her my hat, gloves, and blanket and hesitated, still wearing my coat. She waited.

"I, uh, I have a lot of stuff in my coat. I'll just let it dry."

"Why don't you unload your pockets so we can dry it. It will be much faster."

I reached in a pocket and got the hot cocoa packets. I palmed them and slid them into the back pocket of my jeans. Dani and Mrs. Dodge were waiting.

I looked around. Dani's little backpack was there, fairly stuffed with hundreds of thousands of dollars worth of jewelry.

I grabbed the pliers and slipped them under my coat and into my front pocket. Next I pulled out the batteries, peppermint oil, and matches from the other pocket. The batteries and matches seemed sort of legit, so I handed them to Dani and nodded toward her backpack. She looked at the oil but didn't comment and dropped the stuff into her backpack. I set my phone on the hall table, and reached in for the Spam.

"I was, uh, worried about the stray animals out in the storm so I brought this just in case—but I, I didn't see any."

The Dodges were gracious. They sat us by the fire, fed us, and even let us play with baby Olive before she went to bed. They insisted we stay the night, and solve the dilemma of how to get home in the morning.

Mr. Dodge supplied us with tons of

pillows and blankets, and left us in the living room. Dani and I set up camp, with a comforter draped from the love seat to the couch as our finishing touch.

"We have to go to sleep," I whispered.

"I'm still hungry."

"You already ate most of the crackers," I said, clutching the box.

"Let me have some!"

"I'm hungry too! I walked across Boston!"

"I robbed a house!"

"Shhh!"

We ate crackers, filling our fort with crumbs, and finally fell asleep.

We woke to the sound of Olive's baby screech.

I checked my phone. I'd texted Gloria to let her know what was happening and she must have texted Marco.

Marco: You okay?
Send address

He'd sent the first note around 11 p.m. I guess I didn't hear it come in when Dani and I were bickering over crackers.

The next one said:

Marco: Penny, tell me where you are

I texted him back.

Me: Charlestown
We're fine

Dani texted Hank and Jenny. I didn't ask whether she was confessing to where she really was. When she set her phone on the coffee table I glanced and saw a different text stream just before the screen faded. The heading was "Michael."

"Have you seen Michael yet?" I asked.

"I saw him yesterday before the snow started. He said maybe we could go to New York in a couple of weeks! And he thinks next year I should audition at Juilliard!"

Mr. Dodge came into the room and smiled at our campsite. "Somehow we have more eggs and bread than we could ever eat." He was still looking at the blankets. His lips tightened. Was he trying not to laugh? I sat up and tried to look like an adult. "Way too much toilet paper too," he said. "Anyway, breakfast will be ready soon."

We ate at the kitchen table, looking out at their snow-covered deck. The sun was just up and the skies looked clear. I was ready to conquer the trek home and hoped Dani was feeling strong.

After breakfast another text rang in.

Marco: I'm in Charlestown on the hill

Tell me where you are

He'd successfully forced my hand. I gave him the address and told Dani and the Dodges that Marco was on his way.

Mr. and Mrs. Dodge seemed relieved that a man was coming to assist, and I was annoyed that everyone seemed to think I needed help. I had pliers and batteries and I'd made it there in a blizzard.

We thanked the Dodges profusely as we piled on our layers of dry clothes. We had only just begun to sweat when the handsome prince arrived.

The air was still bitter cold and the snow was deep, but the sun sparkled off it and I knew the walk home would be okay. Marco brought a pair of snowshoes which we strapped on Dani, so she was skimming along easily.

I was both happy to see him and angry that he thought he needed to swoop in and rescue the damsels.

He tried to make conversation, but I was a little monosyllabic. Finally he said, "Penny, I'm not rescuing you. I'm escorting you, that's all."

"I made it from Southie in the blizzard alone!" Why was I on the verge of tears?

"You're amazing. I have every confidence in you. And I wanted to walk you home. Okay?"

He sounded sincere.

"I guess it's okay because here we are, but it's kind of not. You tracked me down like some hunting dog after the fox. Is that what you do? Swoop in and then reap women's gratitude?" My words tasted bitter.

"I wanted to see that you two were okay. Is that so wrong? You must be exhausted after what you did yesterday. Did I mention that was crazy? Not safe!"

"I did what I needed to do and I'm fine. I don't really need your opinion about it and I told you we were okay over text."

Dani had run up ahead and turned back to us with a huge smile. I smiled a little myself, proud of having helped her, happy to see her in a carefree moment.

Marco stopped walking and I stopped

and turned to him. He looked almost boyish in his hat and scarf.

"I'm sorry if I did something wrong," he said. I thought he sounded more like Will than himself. "I care about you and Dani and I was trying to show you that. Maybe I have bad technique. I promise to do better."

He was almost pleading and my stomach turned a little. I had an entirely unpleasant reaction to him in that moment and had to turn away to think. Suddenly I realized that I'd liked his insistent heroics. I wanted to fight with him because I was fighting with myself over him. But even the fighting kept us in a position of action and power. Pleading for forgiveness, promising to be more the way he thought I wanted him, smacked of weakness. But at the same time it was kind, and seemed real, and I'd practically forced him into it by attacking him for coming.

We took up walking again and I shoved the whole complicated thing aside. I'd have to think it through later. For the moment I wanted to make it home without ruining anything permanently.

I took a deep breath, smiled at Marco, and nodded toward Dani. "She's grown up a lot in the past couple of weeks," I said.

"She's quite a young woman." Marco took my gloved hand in his, and we stomped along the hidden Freedom Trail.

CHAPTER SIXTEEN

The roads opened up enough by late afternoon that Hank was able to come get Dani and take her back to Wayland. I hoped he wasn't too tough on her for lying about where she'd been.

Marco was making dinner at his house. I showered, dressed, stripped, dressed, and stripped again, until I was surrounded by nearly everything I owned flung on my bed and floor, and I stood naked in the middle of the mess. I realized I was nervous, really nervous. It was time for me to make up my mind whether it was worth all the emotion he was causing. I couldn't afford all the energy the romantic flip-flopping cost me when I didn't even know what I wanted from a relationship.

I ruled out dresses, then skirts. I tried several pairs of pants and settled on a pair of jeans that made my butt look good. The top was easier: definitely not low-cut, and turquoise brought out the green in my eyes. The final effect was decidedly neutral.

Marco's apartment was every bit Marco. A loft with a modern-eclectic style (I don't know if that's a real thing, but that's what it was). He had a big sectional sofa and a huge industrial-looking coffee table stacked with books underneath and on top. There was an oversized beanbag chair and a huge plastic top-chair, which I later discovered to be an actual top you could sit in and spin around. There was a lot of artwork on his walls, ranging from dour black-and-white photos to children's art. One piece I'd guessed was by a child, an abstract portrait of a red bell pepper, turned out to have been painted by a gorilla named Michael, a friend of the famous Koko. I could definitely hang with a guy who respects gorilla art.

Nothing in Marco's apartment was expected in the sense that I couldn't identify a theme or a traditional way of doing things. The art and furniture weren't placed in the most obvious spots; the combination of pieces was surprising.

I couldn't help thinking of Will's little house outside of Madison. Will's house was expected and comforting. A border of perennials lined the walk up to the door. A porch swing, painted blue to match the trim, hung ready with pillows. Inside overstuffed furniture was arranged in the ordinary way, and art prints hung in traditional places. The kitchen was cozy, with braided rugs and four wooden chairs around a square table. There were earthenware crocks for flour, sugar, coffee, and cookies. There was always a pot of coffee on. It was a masculine version of a grandma's house. Will's house was Tchaikovsky at Christmas. Marco's was cutting-edge jazz, lyrical and dissonant.

Marco kissed me, took the flowers I

offered, and glided across the dark wood floors to the open kitchen on the right. I followed him and climbed up on a high bench on the living room side of the sea-glass kitchen island. He put the flowers in a vase that looked like it was made of paper, poured me a glass of wine, stirred something on the stove, then sat next to me. We toasted each other. It was all going much too smoothly and I had a nervous flutter. He leaned in and kissed me again, longer this time. Smell of balsam, taste of red wine, his face smooth from a fresh shave. I put my arms around him, felt the soft cotton of his shirt and his muscled back beneath. I pulled back and smiled.

"Hungry?" Marco asked with a little irony in his voice.

I tried to look innocent. "A little. Whatever you're cooking smells great."

"My grandfather's puttanesca sauce. I picked up some fresh pasta and bread. I get so bummed about tomatoes this time of year, but I made a wild mushroom salad with some frisée. I hope you like mushrooms. People seem to have strong feelings about them."

"I have the good kind of strong feelings."

"Great." He walked over to a large old-looking wood cabinet, opened it, and turned on some soft jazz. Or I should say some jazz softly, as it certainly wasn't "soft jazz." I wished I knew more about music, as there was some jazz I just adored, but didn't have the words or know the categories. Marco seemed to know what I liked, though, and that was good enough for the time being.

We ate sitting on pillows on the floor at a Japanese-style low table, which made me glad I chose jeans and not a short dress. The table was just off his kitchen, next to a floor-to-ceiling window with a view of his neck of Cambridge.

Spicy sauce—flavors of olives, capers, hot pepper, and tomato. Whole grain bread we dipped in a plate of olive oil with lemon juice and fresh rosemary. The mushroom salad was chilled—earthy mushroom mix, bite of frisée, smooth ricotta salata, black pepper. I wished I could eat more but my stomach was writhing, as if I had wringing hands inside me. I had a bad habit of getting nervous when things went well. I tried to focus on the moment.

"Where did you learn to cook?"

"My whole family cooks—Mom, Dad, grandparents. There was never a question of learning to cook. When I grew up we shopped the European way, of course, visiting the baker, the vegetable stand, the butcher, goat farmer for cheese. I much prefer it that way. We *knew* those people. We visited and heard about what the rain had done to the crop, about the new baby goats, about the butcher's houseful of children. Here I have a harder time finding good ingredients and I know only a few of the people."

I had a little trouble reconciling my very urban Marco with what seemed like a more rural lifestyle. I said so.

"Oh, no. We lived in the city. It's different there. You'll see. I'll take you."

We moved to the living room and dug

through a box of movies, deciding on *City Lights*. The sectional was deep and cozy and the movie short, even if it did leave me in tears. They were consolable tears, and Marco consoled like I'd never been consoled before.

Saturday morning dawned through the windows set high in the exposed brick wall of Marco's bedroom. Marco's side was empty. I registered a little alarm, but was so tired from the night that I let myself drift back to sleep.

When I woke again Marco was there with coffee. I drank it in bed, watching the early light begin to get clearer against the brick of the building next door. I tried to understand what was happening. It was physical (an aftershock of the night before went through me) and I had to admit I felt an emotional pull. Marco had more gravity than some planets.

Dani called that afternoon to thank me for helping her.

"Hank and Jenny put the jewelry in a safe deposit box for me. And they helped me get the boxes from storage so I can go through them. I found my mom's journal from her trip to India."

"When was that, again?"

"It was last spring. She was gone for like two weeks."

"That will be really interesting to read. I'm so glad you're able to begin going through her stuff."

"Uncle Hank has been trying to help Uncle Dob and Aunt Josephine with the trouble with their business. He doesn't tell me anything about the investigations about Brian or my mom. He says the police are working on it, but he doesn't say any more. I don't think they're making any progress."

"Does Dob know you have the jewelry now?"

"No. I begged Hank not to tell him what I did."

"Have you thought more about telling Hank and Jenny about Michael?"

"No! But I'm worried about having to lie to them to go to New York with him." She paused. "But he says his friends are away in traveling shows right now, so I guess it doesn't matter yet. I don't want them to know about him! I really love him and I don't want them to say I can't see him."

I remembered the power of teenage love—in fact, maybe it hadn't changed that much. "I won't tell them," I said, "but I still think you should."

I met Michael the next day at Dani's favorite coffee shop. Dani had talked to Harry and told him about Anita's journals. He asked if she would share them with him and she agreed. She asked me to join her and she wanted to meet for coffee first. I hadn't eaten, so I headed to the coffee shop about an hour early to get some food and hang out until she got there.

I stomped off my boots inside the café door, my eyes already on the menu board. When I looked around for a place to drop my stuff, I saw Dani already at her favorite corner table. She was looking up at a young man standing next to her table. He was thin, not tall, and had wavy hair past his collar. She stood and kissed him and before I knew what was happening he turned to leave. I took a few steps toward him and we met mid–coffee shop.

"Michael," I said. "Why don't you stay a minute? I've been looking forward to meeting you."

Dani came up behind him, her eyes wide with surprise at my untimely arrival.

"This is Penny," she told him. "The social worker I told you about—my friend."

"Please, let's sit," I said.

They shuffled awkwardly back to the table and sat.

"I've heard a lot about you," I began. "You've been a big supporter of Dani's musical theater aspirations."

"She's very talented," he said. He reached for his coffee mug and turned it in circles by the handle on the table in front of him.

"Did you see her in *42nd Street*?"

"I went to a rehearsal. She was real good."

"Why didn't you go to the show?"

"Her mom would have flipped if I went to the performance. She had some grudge against me."

"So where were you that night?"

"I was at my apartment waiting to hear how it went. Why?"

He finally lifted his eyes to me fully. Defiantly.

Dani spoke up. "Michael texted me right after the show—right before I found out Mom was…"

A tear jumped from the corner of her eye and she pushed it away with the back of her hand.

"I have someplace I need to be," he said, standing. "Not that it wasn't fun meeting you and all." His voice was so sarcastic I wished I had a ruler. It was a strange image to have jump to mind, but my mom used to tell me that nuns would smack children's hands with a ruler when they were disrespectful. It had never seemed like a good idea before that moment.

He walked out without another word.

Dani was giving me a death stare. "You're acting like my mom," she said, "but you're not my mom."

"Well, sixteen-year-olds need someone looking out for them, and if you tell Hank and Jenny about Michael I'll leave it to them, but meanwhile somebody should be checking this guy out."

"I can make my own decisions."

We were silent. I still didn't have food and I was famished. I got up and went to the counter to order. When I got back she was focused on her phone and didn't look up.

I waited it out. My food came and I ate, still suffering silence from Dani.

About ten minutes before we were supposed to meet Harry she said, "Let's go."

"Do you still want me along?" I asked.

"Yeah. Because maybe you will have an idea about who killed Mom. Finding out who killed her is more important than you not trusting my judgment."

"It's not that—" I started, but she cut me off.

"Let's just go."

Evidence of Thomas's takeover was everywhere. The wind chime had been replaced by an electronic chime that sounded in the back when we entered. The elegant stuffed chairs were gone and some more contemporary armless seats replaced them. The store looked more like an office and less like a cozy nest where you'd have tea with a friend.

Thomas looked up when we entered. He didn't look surprised so I assumed Harry had told him we were coming. We heard Harry bang in through the back door. He came through the store and greeted us with hugs. He unceremoniously cleared the clutter from the tea table and gestured for Dani to set down the notebook and photos she was carrying. He shuffled off to make tea and we sat. Dani's pile of photos slid over and some fell onto the floor. I picked up two that had landed near my feet. They were both street scenes. Children were frozen by the camera in mid-dance and song. Their bright clothes looked clean, if worn, and I could almost see their long limbs moving to the music. The second photo showed the same scene but captured more of the street vendors behind the children. I could make out red, orange, and yellow necklaces and bracelets hanging on display at one, saris in jewel tones at another, and steam wafting off bowls of something at a third. I longed to sit in the warm sun and smell the spices, to bask in the motherly smile of the woman tending the food.

Harry set out tea, carefully avoiding the pile Dani was rearranging. When he sat, his charcoal corduroy sport coat nearly camouflaged him on the dull new chair. I felt a little chilled and tucked my hands into the sleeves of my sweater. I thought we would look like a gathering of shadows in the corner if anyone walked in. Harry shifted, trying to get comfortable. "Dani, thank you for including us in this. I know it is very personal and very hard. I loved your mother like my own daughter and I love you no less than my own grandchild."

Dani's eyes glistened and she took a deep breath. She glanced my way and it was clear I wasn't forgiven. Maybe I was on some sort of probation. She reached for a pile of photos. "There weren't many pictures of her," Dani began, "but I found this one. I wonder who took it." She passed the photo to Harry, who held it so that Thomas could see. I looked away, already feeling the weight of emotion in the room. Harry handed the photo to me. It showed Anita from the waist up, smiling, squinting just a little in the sun. Her oval face and dark eyes were a mirror of Dani. Anyone who met her on that street that day would know instantly that she was thoughtful and intelligent, that she know how to listen. I set the photo down reverently. Dani was flipping pages in a spiral notebook.

"Here." She began to read aloud:

May fifteenth.

I came here to see my family and to understand our history and the history of the gem industry. I admit I had preconceived notions about the industry, but like so many other things in life, it turns out to be more complicated. Gems have been a part of life in India from before the time when their market value drove so many aspects of society here. Forever, I suppose, gems were discovered as they peeped out of rocks tumbling down the rivers, or exposed from erosion. But before trade became what it is, they were just things of beauty and didn't enrich individuals; they were treasured by communities as proof that life gave precious gifts.

I find it hard to think about their value in a really useful way. In reality, they aren't good for anything (diamonds have found their practical uses, I guess). And yet they are the source of so much effort, so many abuses, so much greed and violence.

Dani paused and drank some tea. She tucked her legs up under her and started again.

May sixteenth.

Today Niles took me to see one of the cutting facilities here. It was more or less clean, if dim and dismal. The work is so precise, so difficult. I couldn't imagine how children could be used for the labor at first, but then realized that they could probably be trained to be quite good at it by twelve or thirteen, and younger children could do much of the processing and polishing work. There were no young children at work at the facility when I visited, although so many people look so young here it's kind of hard to guess ages. Anyway, if it is happening it wouldn't be obvious on my visit.

Children do lots of work in India, much more than children back home. They cook and clean and carry supplies. They care for younger children. I can understand that they have historically been part of the life of gems: digging likely-looking rocks from the mango and coconut groves where rubies and sapphires can be found, sifting through rocks in the river for a glimpse of a jewel. And wouldn't they then have helped to process their finds? To uncover the jewel in the rock?

I can sort of see how children remained a part of the workforce as their communities took on those jobs more formally. It might have been okay—maybe—at first. I don't know. The reports of child labor are horrible in today's world. I asked Niles whether children worked in mining or processing in his operation, and he told me that the laws are different here. I wish he'd been clearer. It's hard to get direct answers from him. I need to learn more. The issues around fair trade fascinate me.

I imagined Anita sitting on a bed in her cousin's house at the end of the day writing her thoughts and struggling to reconcile her preconceptions with the complex reality she saw. Did she talk to her cousins about it again? Could she? Dani flipped a couple of pages and picked up reading.

Tonight after dinner I talked with Niles about the bigger process of sourcing and distribution. I told him how we buy gems that are certified as ethically sourced and processed. He laughed! He told me that there's some traceability for diamonds and even gold, but the vast majority of colored gems are untraceable. Most come from artisanal and small-scale mining and can change hands multiple times before processing. Record keeping is terrible, smuggling is rampant, and corruption abounds. He said that any certification that pretends to trace a gem from source to retail is a lie.

Harry and Thomas looked at each other. Dani and I looked at them. Harry sat forward in his chair and put his elbows on his knees. Thomas ran a hand through his hair. He didn't make eye contact with anyone when he spoke. He said, "I wondered about this. Do you think Anita discovered that our fair-trade certifications are fake?"

I wanted to snatch up the journals and start searching, but we needed to put our heads together. All eyes turned to Dani. "Was there more on this, Dani?" Harry asked.

"I don't think so. This was close to the end. There's a bunch of stuff about food and then she got sick and didn't write much. I think the last pages of the journal are gone because there are those frilly leftover strings of paper in the spiral." She fidgeted with the bits sticking out of the spiral.

That evening I had the apartment to myself to reflect on things. I thought Dani would get over her anger with a little time, so I turned my mind to men. I decided I couldn't let the Marco thing go any farther. It was too intense. Too risky. We had made plans for a weekend away, and I didn't even have a good pulse on him. He was charming and sincere, but too smooth, too mysterious. I still didn't really know if he was telling the truth about Marcella. Then there was all the phone-checking; not that we'd ever agreed not to see other people, but it made me feel too vulnerable. His charming nature was disarming and disturbing at the same time. How much did he really look into my eyes? I had to admit that when he curled against me in the night and pulled me close in his sleep it felt like love. But I didn't think he saw it quite that way when he was awake. If I was just one of his many entertainments I knew my heart couldn't take it.

I decided to focus on Anita's murder. I sat on my bed with a notebook to jot notes as I thought through what we knew so far.

I heard a text come in and grabbed my phone.

Marco: What time can you get away on Friday?
Me: Not sure. Free to talk later?
Marco: Free now?
Me: Ok

It only took him two seconds to call.

"How was your day?" His voice was cheerful but a bit unsure. Sometimes the simplest text can set off alarms.

"Not bad." I tried to sound light and think of something worth reporting. "There was another altercation over a parking spot outside the apartment. The police had to come this time."

Marco chuckled. "Hey, there are some trails about a half hour from the B&B that I thought we might hike Saturday."

"Yeah, about that." I hesitated. I thought about our plan—two nights together, hiking, drinking wine by the fire, waking up next to him. My heart clenched a little and when I tried to breathe through it, it clenched a lot. I recognized that pain and it was exactly what I wanted to avoid. Love-pain. I had to have the courage to escape before I loved him more—before the stage where a breakup would feel like my insides were blackening, crumpling, and sucking my will to live.

"I don't feel right about this," I said.

There was a long pause. I continued, "It's just that, um, this probably can't work. I'm not ready to really get involved and you should be with someone who's, well, not me."

More silence. Long, long silence. I twisted my hair, yanking until it hurt a little.

"Marco, I'm sorry."

"Okay."

Silence. My belly was starting to cramp up. Finally he spoke. "I'm just really trying to hear you. You don't want to do this?"

"I don't really know what I want but I just don't think this is a good idea. I don't think it can end well. I don't want either or both of us to get hurt."

"So we don't try?"

"I'm sorry. I just can't." My insides wanted to cry, but my head was in charge so I stayed stoic. I could even hear it in my voice—

a little tone of efficiency. I didn't want to sound cold, or to be cold, but I couldn't let my emotions loose or I would lose my resolve.

"Okay. I hear you, Penny. You have to do what you think is best."

Regret coursed through me. I could taste it. I could feel the heat of it. All the wonderful possibilities spiraled away from me. The very real memories of his strong hands touching me, our legs tangled in bed—those memories crowded close. *What happens to us?* they demanded. *Can you wish us away? Are we meaningless? Will you rewrite us to make it look like this couldn't be love?*

I blinked hard and swallowed against the lump in my throat. "I'm really sorry. We can talk more later if you want."

"All right, Penny. Bye."

My eyes filled as I put my phone down. I took some deep breaths to ward off the suffocation feeling. I did a mental body check. Breathing, not about to throw up. Must be okay.

Time to refocus.

I pulled out my laptop and one-hand-typed "Gem mining and exportation India."

I read about all the regions of the world that export gems, and learned about the process from mining to processing, cutting, manufacturing, and retail. My vision kept blurring but I wiped away the tears and kept reading. I learned that regulation in the gemstone industry lags behind other extractive industries, like precious metals and diamonds, due to the fragmented nature of the supply chain. Colored gems come from at least fifty countries, and within those countries most of the mining is through small-scale, family-type outfits. These are often in extremely remote locations.

My mind drifted to Marco. In my imagination he texted:

Marco: Can we talk?
Me: Sure. Whenever you have time.
I know you have stuff going on.

Still in my imagination, my phone rang. Marco's smooth voice carried a hint of annoyance. "I have lots of time, Penny. I stopped dating because I was falling in love with you. I don't understand why you had to try so hard to make sure we didn't have a chance for something together."

I shook my head to clear it and reminded myself that even if it's just in your head, a conversation with someone who isn't there is not the best sign of mental health. I wanted another chance but I couldn't go there. Making up a story would just convince me to do something stupid. Marco definitely had plenty of beautiful women around him and in reality he was probably going on a date with one tonight. I felt an inner heave but I held it back. I reasoned that nausea was good for keeping my weight in check.

Returning my attention to the computer, I started reading about child labor in the gem industry. I learned that children are used in mining as well as in the processing centers. They work long hours, preventing them from being able to attend school. If they receive any wages at all, they are extremely low.

However, many children are "bonded" on debts of their relatives and work only to pay those debts. Mine sites are dangerous environments with heavy lifting and risk of exposure to toxic substances like heavy metals, and diseases spread through overcrowding and filthy conditions. In the processing centers they're exposed to dangerous chemicals and lung disease caused by breathing gem dust.

I got up to make a cup of tea, Marco in my head again. "A glass of wine instead, my love? We could forget about everything and watch the stars come out." I ignored him. What else can you do with a voice you made up in the first place?

I took my tea and computer to the couch and started searching again. I searched "corruption in the gem industry." I learned that in addition to horrific labor practices, the gem industry lends itself to smuggling, money laundering, tax avoidance schemes, and forgery. Gems are often used as currency in the drug industry and other illicit trade. Money laundering. Dob.

I thought about what I'd tell Marco if I were giving him the update. How we know Anita was concerned about the gem industry, how her cousin said that the colored stones couldn't be Fair Trade. I would tell him about the child labor, and how I would never, ever buy gems again. He would joke and promise me a vegan-leather wrist wrap when he proposed. I would tell him about all the ways gems are used in corruption and my suspicions about Dob. I would tell him I was

afraid for Dani. He would take me in his arms
—

My fantasy was interrupted by Gloria
banging through the door, loaded down with
bags from a shopping spree. She looked at
me, curled up on the couch with only the glow
of my laptop in the dark room, and said, "Let's
go out and have a glass of wine."

As we were walking out of the
apartment I thought of Marco again, how he
would give me a little kiss and a smile as I
passed through the door. Then it hit me.

When we sat down at a tiny table in the
noisy but not stinky bar a few blocks from our
apartment, I laid it on her. "Gloria, I made
Marco up."

"Yay! You made up with Marco? Wait.
Did you argue?"

"No. I made him up. I just figured this
out. He's been on my mind a lot, you know,
and not just actual memories, but I imagine
what he would say about stuff, what we would
do together. Not all dirty." I smiled to let her
know that I wasn't going to be too intense all
evening. "And now that I think about it, even
when we were dating, I would think about him
when we weren't together—I'd imagine what
he would say or do. I probably have absolutely
no clue who this guy is because I made up
eighty percent of who I believed him to be.
He's probably a drug addict operating an
international trade in young girls online."

"Penny," Gloria said with fake sternness,
"aren't you letting your imagination run a little
wild?"

"I am, Gloria! That's my point. I

imagined him. Not his gorgeous physical self, but who he is, that he could love me, that I might someday love him." Gloria regarded me over the rim of her wineglass.

"If they were of equal sexiness and intelligence, which would you choose," she asked, "a nice guy with just enough bad boy, or a bad boy with just enough nice guy?"

"I don't know," I said, a bit annoyed that she wasn't staying with me on my thought path.

"Sagittarius," she said. "You reserve the freedom not to make up your mind."

I left astrology alone and went back to my line of reasoning. "It's no wonder it never works out for me and guys. That they don't turn out to be what I thought. They never were! I just paint the whole fantasy and then I'm devastated when it comes crashing down. God, it makes so much sense!"

Even Gloria couldn't deny my logic. "Penny, maybe we do idealize people when we fall in love, I don't think anyone would dispute that, but it doesn't mean that they aren't really good, or that they don't really love us."

"Yeah, but how the hell can you know? I clearly don't."

CHAPTER SEVENTEEN

Gloria had emailed Will to tell him about the blizzard, and my accident (and no doubt that I was a complete wreck), and he called on Monday. It was nice to hear him, familiar and steadying with a sweet tone of concern. I poured out the story of the blizzard. It was good to admit to someone that I'd been scared. I told him about Dob and money laundering and Fair Trade and what Anita's cousin had said about colored gems. "But I remember Harry showing me three pamphlets at the shop—one for ethically sourced precious metals, one for diamonds, and one for other gems."

"Why don't we check that out then? See who certified the gems? But Penny, wait until I get there. I'm really scared for you. I have a flight Wednesday afternoon. I'll be there around nine."

"Will…" Damn. I didn't know what to say. "That's so nice, but I'm fine. I'll be extra careful and go places with Gloria and Toryn—"

"Unless you tell me you have something in your love life that will be ruined if I come, I'm coming. I have to know you're safe."

"I, uh, no, nothing like that." I didn't know what else to say. Maybe it would be nice to have the distraction, and the protection. "Thanks, Will. You can stay here if you don't mind the pull-out."

Will arrived Wednesday evening as promised. He visited some friends on Thursday and picked me up at work at five. He was every bit as gorgeous as when I saw him last. I took in his broad shoulders and muscled arms. Despite my earlier reservations I was thrilled to have him there and felt the tug of the old attraction. He lingered in our hello hug and breathed me in. After what had just happened with Marco, I found it a bit overwhelming to be in a romantic head-space again, so I tried to focus on the murder.

We went straight to Mt. Vernon Jewelers. After introductions I got to the purpose of our visit. "Thomas, did you do any research on the sourcing of your jewelry?"

"I did. As you probably know, the Kimberley Process is a real, if imperfect way of tracing the origin of diamonds. There are also processes in place for metals, especially gold, and an organization called Fair Jewelry Action has done a lot of work there." He looked from me to Will and back, shifting from foot to foot. "I wouldn't claim that our diamonds and gold have spotless pasts, but I do feel certain that we've sourced them through organizations that are trying."

He paused and pulled out the three pamphlets I'd already seen and passed them to me, then three to Will. "Pardon my manners, would you like to sit? I'll make tea."

"Thanks, Thomas, tea isn't necessary."

The three of us moved to the new chairs and sat.

"As for the colored gems," he resumed, "I haven't been able to make much progress. My research confirms what Niles said about the lack of traceability. I reached out to our rep, Daniel, at Gems with a Conscience, and left him messages, but he hasn't returned my calls."

I looked at one of the pamphlets in my hand. The tagline read: *Your ethically sound colored gem specialist.* I turned it over and found Daniel's name and number stamped on the back.

"My dad and I are embarrassed and upset about this, I have to admit. I don't know if Anita went down this path. She didn't say anything if she did. I've tried to find this Daniel Trout fellow online, but I can't find him in all the clutter. It seems like every name is common these days."

We thanked Thomas and promised to stay in touch.

Will and I stopped at a bakery at the top of Charles Street for coffee. "I don't feel any closer to figuring this out," I said. "I mean, even if the gems weren't Fair Trade, what does that have to do with Anita? Would someone kill her for finding that out?"

"I don't know," Will said. "We need to follow the trail a bit, though, see if it leads anywhere or not. How can we find out something about this Daniel person?"

"Maybe Toryn can help."

It's good to have connections who are also friends. Toryn did me another huge favor by searching for Daniel on the system at work. When he didn't find anything he traced the incorporation of the business and found a different name. Daniel *Howser* had a record of fraud and money laundering.

Will, Toryn, and I walked along the Esplanade, marveling at the people who took sailboats out in the cold. The wind was harsh along the river and I questioned our decision to walk, but we wanted privacy and it seemed to make sense at the time. I burrowed down into my jacket and looked at Toryn over the collar.

"Howser's business almost certainly isn't legit, you've figured that out," Toryn said. "But it has *a lot* of revenue."

"But it's gems, we would expect that, right?" Will asked.

"Yeah, it's so hard to know what to think when you're talking about such big numbers. But I don't get the sense that this is a well-known organization working with tons of jewelers."

"So this gets us where?" I asked, impatient because it was cold and I was hungry and clueless. "Let's say Daniel is a fraud and Anita found that out. Do we really think he killed her? Would she have invited him into her apartment and accepted food from him knowing he was a crook?"

"Maybe Harry was in on it," Will said.

I shot him a hateful look.

"What if," Toryn said, "Daniel is connected with someone else who knew Anita? Like Chris or Dob, through her dad's business or something? He might have told them that Anita found out and…"

Will and I looked at Toryn and waited.

"…and they had something to lose?" he finished tentatively.

"What?" Will and I chorused.

"Hell if I know." Toryn looked at his shoes. I looked at my shoes. My toes were really cold. I wanted to turn and walk back toward Charles Street, get some Pad Thai. Forget about murder.

Thinking about Beacon Hill made me think about Harry and I dug my phone out of my bag. I dialed the shop and got Thomas.

A few minutes later I hung up and turned around on the Esplanade. Will and Toryn turned with me but then stopped. "Penny, what?" Toryn pleaded.

"Daniel knows Dob," I said. "Thomas said they came into the shop together once, although he doesn't remember why. Everything leads back to Dob."

We put it all together on the walk back. Dob and Daniel did business together and when Anita found out about Daniel's scam, it threatened Dob's business. That probably wasn't hard to do, since Dob was doing illegal stuff. Dob stood to gain control of Dani's trust and the family jewels on top of protecting his business if he just got rid of his sister.

We'd solved the mystery, but had no idea what to do next.

CHAPTER EIGHTEEN

     I called Dani Friday evening to check in. She was upset with Michael, which was good luck for me because she seemed to have let go of her anger with me.

     "I asked Michael if we could go down to New York for this performance at Juilliard," she said. "He was really weird about it so I kept asking questions and, well, I'm not really sure if he actually went to school there." I could hear that she was fidgeting with her phone. "Not that I think he would lie to me, but, well, I'm not sure."

     "Is there a way you can figure that out?"

     "I think I'll try. He doesn't keep a Facebook page or anything, but I'll Google around."

     Her voice was thick and I thought about how hard those teen love relationships are—how hard any relationships are, especially when things get shaky. I decided to change the subject and was debating whether or not to tell her my thoughts about Dob. But before I had the chance, she told me that she was bored hanging out alone because Hank and Jenny were at a fundraiser at the Long Wharf Marriott. "It's a cancer thing, I think. My mom used to go to it every year. I think all their friends do."

I got off the phone as fast as I could without being rude. I told Will, who was in the kitchen working on some snacks. We decided to call Toryn, who loved any excuse to put on tails. Just then Gloria crashed through the door and we told her what was happening. "Oh yeah. It was nuts at the spa today with all the women getting spiffed up for the gala—wait, are you saying…?"

"We're going," Will said.

Gloria and I headed to our bedrooms to dig out dresses and poor Will dug around to figure out the nicest things he'd brought. He was way too big to borrow from Toryn, so he was just going to look like someone's shabby date. He clearly wanted that someone to be me, but I still didn't want to think too much about romance. We didn't know how we were going to get in, exactly, but that was just a detail.

When Toryn arrived we piled out the door. We took the T down to the waterfront and walked over to the Marriott. There were loads of people mingling in the ballroom foyer, and we were able to blend in easily enough, although we would need to show tickets to get into the ballroom. I scanned the crowd and found Hank and Jenny. I turned my back to them and kept looking around. I saw Dob and Josephine talking with some people over by one of the portable bars, and Jill not far from them, talking with an older man.

My entire plan consisted of using the element of surprise to get Dob to confess to murdering Anita. Some might say it was not well thought out, but things were moving quickly and I had to do something.

I glanced at my friends and took off toward the bar. When Dob saw me coming his mouth opened, but before he had a chance to say anything I leaned in close and said, "How could you do it, Dob? She was your sister! I know what you did and I know why and you're not going to get away with it."

Dob turned pale before flushing red. I had the attention of quite a few people close by, including Jill, who had stopped her conversation and turned to watch.

"You are insane, Ms. Wade," he growled. "You just keep coming back. Now you're accusing me of murdering my sister?"

"I am," I snarled. Dani had been through too much and all because of this man's greed. "You found out she knew about Daniel Howser's scheme and you were so greedy and fearful of getting busted for your own illegal schemes that you just took care of the problem, didn't you?"

Josephine's mouth was hanging open and Jill stepped closer.

"I will tell you once, so that you will go away and stop making a scene, Ms. Wade. I did not kill Anita. I didn't even see her that night."

Hank and Jenny had come up behind me. I didn't realize it until I heard Hank's voice. "Dob was at a dinner, Penny. You need to leave this to the police."

"He left!" Jill's voice hit a pitch that grabbed the attention of several other party guests. "He stepped out of that dinner."

"That's a lie and you know it! It was you who arrived an hour late," Dob hissed. "Where the hell were you? Would you care to explain that to Chief Dorian here?"

Josephine looked back and forth between her husband and Jill, getting redder by the minute.

"Where were you, Jill?" Hank's voice was reasonable and I was surprised that he was engaging, but I guess a good cop would never waste an emotional moment like this. Dob, Josephine, and Jill all looked like they were about to crack.

"I was taking care of personal business," Jill spat. "I've told the police, I don't need to explain myself to you."

"A personal vendetta, you mean?" Dob nearly yelled. "That's why you got involved with me, isn't it? To get back at Anita for what happened to Josh? But she didn't care, because she really didn't care about me, so you didn't get your satisfaction, did you?"

I was totally lost. Dob and Jill were having an affair? Who was Josh? And what did this have to do with gems or money laundering or Daniel Howser?

I had to trip Dob up.

"You stole the gems, Dob. You can't deny having them."

"They belong to my family!"

"They belong to Dani."

"Dani is my family!"

"Did you take them the night you killed Anita?"

Dob reddened again and I felt Hank's

hand grasp my arm from behind. I wrenched it away.

"There's a—"

I was interrupted by a huge crash. We all turned to see the giant floral display spilled on the floor, the vase shattered. Toryn was edging away.

His eyes flicked to me.

I turned back to the gathering of suspects.

Gloria stepped forward, looking at Dob. "Did Anita object to your affair with Jill? Did she threaten to tell Josephine?" Leave it to Gloria to latch onto the affair.

"I knew."

All heads snapped to Josephine. She shrugged a little. "I didn't really care. It took the pressure off me having to have sex with him."

We all paused for a few beats on that one.

Hank stepped forward to take control of the situation, but Dob spoke first. "Look, this has been awful for everyone, but wild accusations aren't going to help. I loved my sister. I would never hurt her." He blinked and swallowed hard. "You don't have to believe me, but you do need to leave now."

I wasn't ready to leave without an answer, and I was starting to believe Dob.

"Well, somebody—"

"Somebody needs to remove you and your friends from this hotel!" Jill's eyes were ablaze.

"Where's security?" Dob was looking at Hank.

"Look," I said, "we have to figure this out before someone else gets killed." Will had stepped to my side. "We all love Dani and she needs—"

"Ma'am?" It was a hotel security guy trying to puff up his skinny chest. "Are you an official guest of this event?"

"Uh…"

Will spoke up. "We came to enlist the help of some friends on an important matter."

"Please answer my question, ma'am." He ignored Will.

"I, uh, lost my ticket but I should be on the list. You can go check."

"Please come with me, ma'am, and you too, sir."

We started to walk with the officer and I realized that all of the guests were staring. I hoped Vivian wasn't there. I hoped they were all just strangers bussed in for the event and I'd never see them again because they were all going back to Boise. My face was hot, but less with embarrassment than failure-shame.

I looked around for Gloria and found her beaming up at a handsome guy, deep in conversation.

We met up with Toryn at security. He assured them the floral thing was an accident and they escorted the three of us from the building.

I had time to think on Sunday as I drove north in Toryn's Mercedes, escaping Boston for a little while. I had no idea what to do to help find Anita's killer, and I needed some space.

Once I was out of town the landscape opened up. There were enough evergreens to keep the snowy drab winterscape from flattening out entirely. I realized that the holidays were coming, that time was marching along while I was almost too busy to notice. Dani must be thinking about the holidays too, and how different they would be this year. Her mom's apartment was packed up and in storage and she was in total limbo.

The heat in the old Mercedes wasn't working very well so I was still bundled in my coat, hat, and mittens. I jittered my legs and wiggled in my seat. I pulled my hat down farther over my ears.

I hadn't yet learned to keep my mind off Marco. Maybe part of me didn't want to, but I needed to.

My obsessive Marco distraction made me feel disloyal to Will, but I wasn't dating Will and twelve years of dreaming about him didn't make it a commitment. Will made me laugh, he was a great cook, he liked to talk about my work, and he knew my history. He was the kind of guy who would ask if I found it patronizing if he opened the door for me.

Marco tasted the wine and opened the door. And I'd basked in the attention.

I flipped through radio stations and stopped on a country station. I rumbled along in the cold singing "she's my kind of rain; like love from a drunken sky; confetti falling down all night; she's my kind of rain." I imagined Marco singing love like that to me. I glided into the fantasy until I caught myself and jerked the car back onto the road.

The girls burst out of the back door when I pulled up to Owen's shingle-sided house. It wasn't a typical farm house; it was big, with a swimming pool and huge windows for taking in the mountain views. I wondered if the girls' enthusiasm was mostly about me or the bag of gifts. I'd had to call to get sizes; they were growing so damn fast. In my bag I had four Life Is Good T-shirts: one blue size 10-12 "Peace, Love, Soccer" for Morgan; light pink size 8-10 with a flower butterfly for Lizzy; purple size 6 stripy heart for Claire; and a little dark pink sleepy kitty in size 3T for Ava.

The kitchen smelled of fresh corn tortillas. I stopped and took a deep breath and looked around. There was an entire wall of the girls' artwork, the bright colors in lively interaction with the rest of the kitchen and dining area. Maria had brought a bit of Costa Rica with her to New Hampshire. Bright pottery, cheery reds and oranges on the walls and cabinets, and varnished wood furniture created a warm and festive kitchen worthy of the noise and life always dancing around it. Owen and Maria greeted me with hugs. They had created the kind of home Owen and I had always longed for, and I wondered how much that filled the hole for Owen.

When breakfast was served I sat down between Ava and Morgan. Ava peered into her juice and called to her mom, "What happened to my *big* ice cubes? I just have little ones!" This gained her a chuckle and an explanation and I realized that by girl four, parents probably got desensitized to the humor.

Morgan loaded my plate with gallo pinto, eggs, fried plantain, and tortillas. She was big sister caregiver—I knew a lot about that.

I looked around the table at the busyness and smelled the food and decided to stay forever. I could build out a room in the barn or something. Or maybe it was my stomach talking. I'd been known to make rash decisions influenced by food, and fresh tortillas were highly persuasive.

Owen showed no better resistance to the tortillas. He had widened into nearly twice the brother I'd had ten years ago. It was as if each of the four pregnancies enlarged both Owen and Maria a bit, so that with each child they could offer more lap space and bigger hugs. Their hearts grew right along with their bodies and I'd never seen Owen so at home with himself.

The girls chattered on about soccer and their new puppy, the finer points of Santa, and which of their sleds was the fastest. Owen moved a bit closer to me. "How's work?"

"It's okay. A lot to handle really, but your chaos makes my life seem tame, though not as much fun." I was determined to stay off the subject of Dani. "Can we go see the alpacas after breakfast? Do they spit or something?" I asked. They were a relatively new addition to the farm and I hadn't been there to see them yet.

Lizzy spoke up. "We have six now! They don't spit. We got a new baby last month!"

I adored all four of my nieces, but Lizzy really tore at my heart. She was the image of the sister Owen and I had lost. I swallowed against the lump in my throat.

After breakfast we headed down to the fields and Owen and I had a few minutes to catch up while the girls ran and climbed and jumped and sang.

"Owen, this is kind of a hard question to ask, but when I see Lizzy I see Sarah and I know you must too. How do you deal with that?"

"I see Sarah but I mostly see Lizzy," he said. "I guess I've just come to terms with it. I used to try not to think about Sarah, but having Lizzy showed me that it was a waste to throw away the memory and that it didn't really protect me in the end. Now when Sarah comes to mind I just smile and enjoy Lizzy because she is here and now and very much her own person and also a living tribute to Sarah."

"Does she know about Sarah?"

"She does. I show the kids old pictures and she knows that she looks like the sister I lost. Of course I haven't told her how many freaky similarities there are, because that would seem unfair to her individuality."

"You're a great dad, Owen. I don't know where you got it."

"Thank God it turns out you don't have to have a good parent to be one. Might have made it easier though." He chuckled. "But I get the chance to invent fatherhood on my own, knowing I don't want to be like Dad. A lot of people just do what their parents did, ya know? I'm doing it fresh. Ziplock Fresh." He laughed and nodded toward the girls.

Morgan was brushing an alpaca while Lizzy and Claire were climbing on the fence. Little Ava was squatting down digging in some dirt. We could see her mouth moving, but couldn't hear what she was saying. I inched closer until I could hear her song amidst the chatter of her sisters. She was singing, "I'm a hamster princess; I love to play in dirt. I'm a hamster princess."

Owen came up behind me. "That's a new one. Maybe we should make a Habitrail castle for her."

I resumed plotting to stay forever.

CHAPTER NINETEEN

Dani called as I drove back into town. She was crying.

"I did a bunch of research," she stammered, "and Michael isn't in any graduating class from Juilliard for the past four years. I also can't find his name associated with *Elf*—that's the show he said he was in."

"Did you ask him directly?"

"I did and he got really mad and stopped answering my texts. Now he won't text me." She sniffled a few times and continued, "I don't know if I did something really wrong or if he lied to me the whole time. Either way is horrible!"

"I know it doesn't help, but you wouldn't be the first girl to believe a guy's lies."

By this time I was sitting in Toryn's parking spot with the car turned off. Freezing.

"Do you need anything?" I asked. "Have you talked to Jenny about this?"

"No to both," she said. "I'm mostly angry but I'm glad I found out. I don't want a guy who's a total fraud! I'm gonna get over it."

She was still crying but sounded a little steadier. I believed that she would get over it and move on, and I told her so, and before we hung up I extracted a promise that she'd call if she needed me.

When I got home, Will was in the kitchen stirring risotto, his new specialty, and reading a book on Boston Revolutionary War sites. He'd spent the day sightseeing.

Gloria was out on a date.

Will poured some wine for me and put down his book. I sat at the breakfast bar, nervous because the scene seemed so romantic. I was tired and still thinking about my day with Owen and his family.

"You know, Owen and I really plowed through the cleanout of our childhood home. I brought home two boxes that I'd stored in the basement before I moved out. I haven't opened them."

"It'll probably take a while for you to process it all, huh?"

"Yeah, I mean, we had to be efficient and it was really emotional, but we just dealt with that and kept forward momentum. We had to get the house empty so we could put it on the market."

"Was it sad?"

"A lot of the memories were sad, especially Sarah, but I'm not sad to be rid of the house. Who wouldn't want to slough off their unhappy-childhood home? I *was* sad that Owen wouldn't agree to burning it down."

Will nodded and kept stirring.

"Do you think there are patterns from our past, like ruts, that we can't escape?" I asked.

"No."

"Do you think if we run away from the past we get into trouble?"

"I think we need to acknowledge the past."

"Then we can flip it the bird and run away?"

"Yeah, if that's how you want to handle it."

"I think I threw the baby out with the bath water."

"Whaddya mean?"

"Sarah. Trying to forget everything meant I couldn't hold my memories of her. I think she would want me to. And—I think I want to."

I was crying just a little, but it was as much relief as sadness. I shifted around on my stool and poked a cracker at the cheese Will had set out.

I watched as Will set the table. He saw me cock my head a little when he added candles.

"I just want the table to be nice, okay?"

"Sorry. It is nice."

Will brought out salad, risotto, and bread. We sat.

"What if Anita was like me? What if her childhood kind of sucked and she just wanted to get away from it?"

"Lots of people do."

"Both her brother and her ex spun off parts of her dad's business, which was at least moderately lucrative. Why didn't she? She didn't even source gems through her family in India."

"Hmm." Will glanced at my plate.

"It's delicious. You nailed the risotto. I would never have the patience. I'm just talking too much. I'll eat."

We ate in silence for a few minutes. Darkness was settling in and lights came on in the building next door.

"Her dad didn't die that long ago. I think it was like a year. Then she went to India a few months later."

"Would there be a connection?"

"Maybe she realized that she's next," I said. "The next generation. The next to die. Maybe she wanted to face up to her family history, or see if she could understand things differently."

I ate some salad, then sat back in my chair cradling my wine glass.

"I don't think her dad left much to Dob," I said. "He'd probably already proved himself as a lousy business person."

"That seems likely," Will said, "it was only a year ago after all."

"What if her dad left her more than the gems and a stock portfolio?" I stood and started pacing. "What if he left her a share in the family business in Jaipur?" I stopped pacing and looked at the lights out the window.

"Will you sit down a minute?" Will asked.

I did.

"I know this is really important, and I want to help you get it resolved for your safety and Dani's." He took a long breath and I felt suddenly nervous in the serious air. "When it's all over, why don't you come back to

Madison with me?"

I didn't move, just watched his face and tried to figure out what I was feeling.

He continued, "You could do social work there if you want, or I could support us and we could start a family. I know you want kids and I do too."

I shifted in my chair and looked at the two of us reflected in the window with the neighbors' lights beyond breaking into the image.

"I think I want kids," I said, "but I don't know if I'd be a good mom." I crossed my legs, uncrossed them, then leaned on the table. "I love Boston and I also love the idea of a beautiful home in the country with dogs and kids and mud."

"Then consider it?"

I thought I was off the hook for the moment, but he went on. "I know you would be a great mom, and I'd be a great dad and husband. I love you, Penny."

My elbows were still on the table and I caught myself before I put my head in my hands. Instead I turned and looked at him. His eyes were soft but not pleading, and I knew he believed in the house and the three kids and the golden retriever and the treehouse and cantaloupe in the garden. I believed that some people could have that, but I didn't know if I was one of them, and at that very moment in time, sitting at my table in South Boston, I was not one of those people. I was living paycheck to paycheck, trying to solve a murder and stay alive. I was trying to help other people's children. Giving that up for my own felt selfish and, well, distant at best. I took a deep breath, slowly so he wouldn't see me struggling.

"It's lovely to think about. I will keep thinking about it. I need to get through this chapter of things right now."

His lips turned up a little but his eyes stayed steady.

"I'm so distracted," I said, "and I know you understand that. I'm really glad you're here with me and I'm glad you told me how you feel. I wish I were as clear as you are. Maybe I will be soon."

I rose from the table and he stood too. I stepped to him and he put his arms around me. We stood there for a long time and I wasn't sure whether my heart was pounding over him or anxiety about solving the murder. I slid out of his arms and gave him what I hoped was a reassuring smile.

"I need to call Hank. We'll talk more about this soon."

"Of course." I could see he was disappointed, but I also knew he understood my urgency about Dani.

Hank picked up on the fourth ring. "It's Penny. I was thinking, did Anita inherit part of the business in Jaipur when her dad died?" I'd jumped in without formalities.

"Penny. After the debacle at the gala, I'd hoped you would let this go and allow the police to follow through."

"Please? I've been thinking about Anita. I'm not crashing parties or endangering Dani. I'm just thinking."

"The police are considering who may

have had an interest in Anita's assets, but her will left everything to Dani. An interest in the business couldn't be stolen by a murderer."

"So she did have a share. Was it big?"

"This isn't for discussion."

"Does Dani know about it?"

"Penny."

"Please, Hank. If you don't tell me I'll just have to ask her and if she doesn't know and you or Dob don't want her to know, well, then she'll find out."

"No. She doesn't know. She's only sixteen and the will didn't specify an age at which she would be given her part of ownership. We're working with the lawyer to figure out what to do."

"So she may own her part already," I said.

Hank was silent.

"Thanks, Hank." I tried to sound nonchalant. "I'll call you if the urge for mischief strikes."

"That's a good idea."

Will was in the kitchen cleaning up.

"Wanna watch a movie?" he asked. "Or go out for a stroll and a drink?"

I looked at him and he backed away. "Sorry," I said. "I was thinking and kinda couldn't hear you and think. What did you say?"

"I asked if you want to go for a walk or watch a movie."

"Oh. No." I tried to go back to my train of thought but he was still looking at me. He was trying to be a good sport and leave the seriousness at dinner behind and I was being totally inconsiderate. "I mean, maybe a little later."

Will smiled. "We could have a drink at the wine bar and then watch a classic, or maybe some Monty Python?"

"Yeah." I really needed to think.

"I'll finish the kitchen and—"

"Will," I snapped, "hang on. I can't think."

He saw the look on my face and stopped. He motioned zipping his lip. He went back to the kitchen.

Sweet guy. Talked too much. And that was all I needed to jog my brain back to where I'd been headed. I needed to talk to Harry.

Nobody would be at the shop this late. I had to make up an excuse to get his cell number from Dani.

I dialed her.

"Hey, Penny! Guess what! I'm at the Four Seasons! Leena and Niles invited me to stay in their penthouse here for a few days since it's winter break. I get to swim in the pool and do stuff downtown and go shopping with Leena and be really spoiled!"

I tried to think what I could say that wouldn't sound weird or forced. Nothing came out.

"Penny?"

"Yeah, sorry, I'm here. That's really fun! Hey, I was wondering if you have Harry's cell number? I just wanted to, uh, call him."

"Nope." Dani was too cheerful to question what I was up to. "But here I am right across the Garden from Beacon Hill! I can ask Leena if I can go visit him tomorrow and meet you there? That would be fun."

"Okay," if it was the best I could get. "When?"

"Can you go on your lunch at noon? I'll text you after I talk to Leena."

I had a lot of trouble going to sleep. Stuff was niggling at my brain but I couldn't catch it. I hated the idea of Dani with Niles and Leena. Was I just jealous of Leena for getting Dani's affection?

CHAPTER TWENTY

Will had coffee made and was flipping pancakes when I went out to the kitchen. Gloria was still out. I got a text from Dani early.

Dani: Leena made plans for us already. Sorry. I'll call soon.

I called Hank. "We have to get her out of there."

"Where? What now?"

"We need to get Dani back. Niles killed Anita and Brian."

"Penny..."

I knew I must sound insane now after accusing Dob at the gala. But this time I was sure, and I had to convince Hank. "Listen to me. Anita never wanted a part of the family business and when her dad died it was foisted on her. She faced the obligation and went to Jaipur but she didn't like what she saw. Niles was dependent on her as a partial owner and as the key to US business. Whatever Dob is doing isn't the kind of legitimate outlet Niles is looking for, but I'd put money on Niles being a big piece of Dob's legal problems.

"Anita figured it out: the illegal trade, the problems with the business in Jaipur. She wasn't going to play it Niles's way. She was on the verge of blowing the whistle."

I paused to catch my breath, hoping for a sign that Hank wouldn't shut me down completely. He was silent.

"Niles is so identified with the family business that he even took the name Nayak. What Englishman takes his Indian wife's surname? He wanted to preserve the business, preserve the fortune, save his reputation and his way of life. Anita was going to destroy that."

"Penny, Niles was in London when Anita died."

"Did you verify that? He said he was in London, that's all, right?"

"I can have the detectives verify if they haven't already."

"Great. But Hank, I don't know if Leena knows the plan, but Niles is trying to take Dani and use her to get what he wants with the business—he can't risk her acting like Anita, so he either has to get her share from her somehow or use her as a puppet. That's why they have been trying to persuade her to come to India, and spoiling her, and calling her Princess."

Hank sighed through the phone. "I don't know if you're right, but I'm going to look into Niles's whereabouts just in case."

I fidgeted and picked at my pancakes but remembered to thank Will for breakfast. We didn't talk a lot at the table. Probably because I'd brought a notepad and was jotting down thoughts.

After breakfast Will was ready to leave for the airport. He probably couldn't tell from how I'd been acting, but I really would miss him. He pulled me in for a hug and I laid my head on his shoulder.

"I'll think about what you said. I really will."

"Maybe you can come visit Madison soon?"

"Yeah, I'd like that."

I lifted my head from his shoulder, and he kissed me. One long, sweet kiss that could have gone passionate, but we both knew it wasn't the right moment.

Twenty minutes later my phone rang. "A car was rented at BOS in the Nayaks' company name the day before Anita died. It isn't conclusive, but it's something."

"Was he here when Brian was hit?"

"They didn't find a record of him here then."

We were silent for a minute.

"Hank, we can't take a chance. They have Dani."

"I know." I could hear his irritation.

"She wanted to meet me at Harry's shop today but Leena told her no." I took a deep breath and tried to think what else the detectives could check. "Does Dani have a passport?"

"I don't know. I don't think she's ever been out of the country, so probably not."

"Could you check—"

"Yes."

I picked at my fingernails and rubbed lotion on my hives, and paced for about thirty minutes until he called back.

"Chris has submitted an application for a passport for Dani."

"Do you think he's in on this?"

"I don't know if there's anything to be 'in on.' I'm willing to bet he's clueless and Niles or Leena persuaded him to get her a passport so that she could go for a visit."

"Where is it in the process?"

"The application was for expedited approval. It'll be ready tomorrow."

"Flights?"

"The three of them are booked for tomorrow evening."

"Can they just take her?"

"Either Chris agreed or they're betting he won't send the authorities after them."

"Hank—"

"Penny, I've loved her longer than you have. I'm doing my best. If you thought it would be hard to get me to take this seriously, think about how hard it will be for me to get the detective in charge to listen. I know we don't have much time. I'm driving downtown now. Let me go do what I can."

"Don't let the police go there."

"What?"

"I want Dani safe before anyone confronts Niles."

"The police will—"

"He killed two people, Hank, even if he hired a hit on Brian or whatever. I know you trust the police. Fine. But I don't trust Niles. I want her away from them first."

"I'll call you when I have anything."

I didn't get to call the shots for the police. Go figure.

I called Toryn and brought him up to speed.

"I'm dyin'. All I can do is sit on my hands and wait. Oh, and I'm supposed to be on my way to work by now." I'd been thinking all night about what to do about work. I'd used up all my free passes. I'd screwed up repeatedly and I was going to have to choose whether to quit or get fired (or abandon the Dani case, which was clearly not going to happen).

"I'll come over. Or you can come here. Or we could both go there." He was talking quickly.

"To work?"

"No, the Four Seasons."

"And what?"

"And find her? And wait in the lobby? And drink tea and look out at the Public Garden? Hell, I don't know, Penny! We could do *something*."

"Okay. Let's meet at Downtown Crossing in an hour." I had to do something about work.

I called Nathan and caught him before his first client. I told him the highlights. "So you're just waiting now, right?" he asked. "Can you wait it out at work and just keep your phone on?"

"I can't help anyone today, Nathan. There's no way I can be attentive. I would just do more harm than good."

"Call Lynnie and tell her you're taking a mental health day."

"I've made too many excuses already. My clients aren't getting the attention they need, and Vivian isn't going to keep letting things go." I stopped talking and picked at the seam of my jeans. "I have to quit. I'll call Vivian."

Sweet Nathan tried to talk me out of it, but I'd made up my mind because I knew the alternative was getting fired anyway and I still didn't know how much longer Dani would need me away from work. I called Vivian and told her I was resigning. She accepted my resignation with some platitudes wishing me well. Efficient, businesslike.

I would have to set aside some time to think about how I was going to pay the rent and feed myself, but first I needed to get Dani safe.

"What if they see us?" I said to Toryn as we walked across the Common, from the Downtown Crossing to the Four Seasons. "What if we tip them off and they do something stupid?"

"Okay, we need a plan," he said. "We shouldn't sit in the lobby. Let's go into Bristol and I'll act straight and we can ask for a secluded table."

I liked the idea. "We won't be able to see much, but we're mostly just waiting for Hank to call anyway."

"Right. And we can drink a lot and if we're there a long time we can have tea. And scones."

"Tea sandwiches."

"Cake."

We reached the entrance and sobered a bit. I looked around, Toryn looked around. We didn't see anyone we knew.

We sped up to the host stand, Toryn affecting a strange, stiff swagger. He puffed up his chest and lowered his voice. "Table for two please. We'd like something a bit private if we may." The hostess led us to a relatively sheltered table. We ordered mimosas.

I regretted that choice almost instantly. I could see the table where Marco and I had sat. There was a beautiful couple there sharing a fruit plate.

"Part of me regrets breaking up with Marco, but it was the right thing to do."

"He was darling, but you have to do whatever your psychopathic inner guide tells you."

"It changes its mind a lot."

"That's because hope springs eternal."

"Hope eternally springs leaks."

"And we eternally plug them up."

"True. Hope is relentless."

We drank and waited and drank some more and waited and drank and then ordered some food because we were getting drunk.

My phone finally rang just as our food arrived.

"Hank! What's happening?"

"We have enough to take Niles in for questioning."

"I have an idea about how to get Dani," I said.

"Okay…" He was definitely hesitant. After all my great ideas!

"As far as anyone knows, Dani is happy to be there and you and Jenny and Dob and I are all clueless, so we have to find a way that looks normal. They're clearly not letting her dash off with friends, but if they're pretending to care about her welfare and acting all parental, they would have to let her go to the doctor."

"The doctor."

"I'll text Dani just to say 'hey, how's it going?' then right after that I'll block my number and text again like a doctor appointment confirmation."

"We could name a doctor at Jenny's old clinic," Hank added. "I think Dani would recognize the name of the clinic."

"So she'd have two tip-offs. She's smart, Hank, and we have to bank on her trusting us."

"I'll talk it over with the detective here and see if we come up with a better plan."

I kind of hoped they would.

There we were. Day drinking at the Bristol.

We picked at our food in silence but I didn't feel any more sober. In fact, my face felt pretty hot and I was a bit swimmy. It flashed through my mind that at least the Bristol's bathrooms were really clean and nice.

Toryn had some ideas. "We could just go up there and get her."

"The desk doesn't give out room numbers."

"Text her."

"That couldn't end in disaster," I quipped.

"Fine. We could have the desk call up and tell them that friends left a credit at

Bristol for their lunch. Then when they come down, we grab her and run."

The waiter, Eric, came with more bread and Toryn commented on his buns. Eric accepted the corny compliment and asked Toryn if there was anything else he would like. Toryn said that there was, and the flirty banter deepened. I watched the two of them in disbelief. Dani was in danger, these two were virtual strangers to each other, and romance was blooming over a basket of bread.

I checked my phone. I kicked Toryn under the table. I went to the bathroom and they were still bantering when I came back.

"The least you can do is bring me a free drink," I said to Eric, "for stealing my date."

He reddened and rushed off.

"What'd you do that for?" Toryn demanded.

"For a drink."

Eric returned with drinks for both of us.

Toryn said, "My friend was just giving you a hard time. She's dense, but she never thought I was straight."

"It's okay, as long as you give me your number." Toryn gave Eric his number and he called Toryn's cell.

"Now you have mine too."

Toryn beamed.

Eric left to attend his other customers.

We drank and waited for Hank to call. He didn't.

"Nobody's thought of a better plan because my plan's the best." Either my speech was slurred or my ears were a little sluggish. "I'm the planner, the plan wo-*man*, I'm gonna save the girl."

Toryn gave me a blank stare and pulled out his phone. He typed something and looked at the end of the bar where Eric was standing. Eric pulled his phone out of his pocket, looked at it, smiled, and looked over at Toryn.

I couldn't watch anymore, so I gazed out the window at the Public Garden. Two police cruisers pulled up and double parked outside. I looked at Toryn.

We left cash on the table for Eric and went out to the lobby.

Two officers were entering the building. We tried to move close to the front desk to eavesdrop.

Just at that moment Niles, Leena, and Dani came into the lobby from the elevators with their bags. Niles was looking totally incognito in a hat and dark glasses.

Toryn and I ducked behind the giant floral arrangement in the middle of the lobby.

Dani looked tense. She looked around and her eyes widened when she saw me. She started toward us, and I motioned her to stop. Niles caught her moving away out of the corner of his eye and called her over. He was keeping her on a tight leash.

The police officers were at the desk speaking to a manager and I saw Niles look over at them. I still didn't know if the officers were there for him or not. Wouldn't Hank have let me know? I wasn't taking chances and Niles looked jumpy.

"Distraction," I said to Toryn, and I moved toward Dani. Toryn went with his now-signature move and tipped the table where we'd been sheltered behind the nine-foot floral arrangement.

I ran right into the trajectory of the giant glass bowl and it hit me just as I got close enough to call to Dani, "Taxi—now—go!"

The bowl took me down.

Dani dashed for the door to the driveway where taxis are always ready.

Leena started to follow her but I got halfway back up and lunged for her ankle.

The police still hadn't figured out who Niles was, if they were even there for Niles. I heard Toryn cry out, "Officer, that man accosted me—that's him!" He was pointing to Niles, who looked utterly shocked and tried to run. An officer caught his arm and detained him.

I had no idea what to do with Leena's ankle, but she solved the problem for me by screaming and pulling away.

I pulled myself up so I could see the door. Dani had made it out. Leena ran out behind her.

Toryn was continuing his scene, waving his hands wildly at the officer. "His name is Niles Nayak and he's a fiend. An absolute abuser, I tell you. I've never been so humiliated." He had on his gayest affect. Niles looked stupefied. "I do *not* want to tell you the details in this public place, but believe me, it's not pretty."

I still didn't know if the police were there for Niles, so I dialed Hank. There was some blood on my phone and I wondered where it had come from. It was annoying because it made it hard to work my touch screen. I finally got through.

"Hank, I'm at the Four Seasons. Did the police come for Niles? They're here."

"They have it handled. I'm almost there." He hung up.

I went over and wedged myself between the officer and Niles. "Remember me?" I said.

I could tell by his face that he did, so I went on.

"Two out of three ain't bad, but you didn't get me. I keep on survivin'!" I couldn't believe the venom in my own voice. I took one step away and turned. I looked at Toryn, who was smirking.

"You just quoted Meatloaf and Destiny's Child in like one sentence," he said.

"Five points for you," I retorted.

Hank burst through the door, looked at the disaster on the floor. Looked at me, frowned. Then, "Where's Dani?"

"I sent her off in a cab."

"Where?"

"I don't know." Big detail.

Hank stepped close to the officer and Niles. Toryn took my arm and pulled me aside.

"You're covered in blood," he said calmly.

I looked down. I was. And I'd landed on the cast arm, which was throbbing. "I think it's all just little cuts." One leg was bleeding pretty fiercely. "And maybe one sorta big one."

Hotel security had come out and while two of them joined the conversation with the police, a third brought a first-aid kit and started fussing over me.

When I was all wrapped up it started to sink in and I had to sit. I borrowed Toryn's coat so I wouldn't get blood from my clothes on their fancy upholstery.

I took a couple of deep breaths and looked around.

I felt my phone vibrate and pulled it out.

Dani: Thanks Penny
I'm headed to Wayland
Leena is with me she's ok

The police, Hank, and Niles left. I thought Hank could have at least nodded in our direction.

"They're going to plan a parade for us," I said. Then Toryn took me to the ER for stitches.

After the ER ordeal, we took the T back to my place.

Toryn updated Gloria while I called Dani.

"Penny, it was scary!"

"Good job getting out of there."

"I mean even before that. Niles and Leena were planning to take me to India! But Leena didn't do anything wrong or anything. She just wanted to take me home."

"The detectives said there were tickets booked for tomorrow. Why were you leaving today?"

"Niles had told Leena to keep the trip a surprise for me. But she took me shopping and stuff and I'm not sure if she let it slip on accident or just thought I deserved to know. Leena's really nice." Dani was talking fast but she sounded strong. "I told her I didn't want to go. Or that I did, but not now. So when we got back to the hotel she told Niles that, and he got really mad and said we were going right away because he'd gotten my passport and was going to change the flights."

I'd put my phone on speaker so Toryn and Gloria could hear. We were all staring at it in amazement.

"I was planning to tell a security person at the airport. I didn't want to try to get away before that."

"Dani, you're one brave, smart girl." I still didn't know if she knew that Niles had killed her mom and Brian. I was thinking about that when she solved the problem for me.

"Where's Hank? I saw him running into the building when I left. How did he know?"

"We put some pieces together that kind of made the police want to ask Niles some questions, so the police went to the hotel to do that."

"Did Niles kill my mom?"

I took a deep breath. "I think so."

Hank and Jenny had a giant Douglas fir in their living room and had invited me to join them on Christmas Eve. They'd gone overboard with decorating and baking, and Dani was helping in the kitchen and playing hostess. She seemed taller than she had just weeks before.

She handed me a glass of wine and plopped down on the sofa. Perry the cat had joined the household and he jumped up beside her.

"Guess what? I'm going to India!"

"*What?*"

"Not until summer, but Leena invited me and I want to go. She'll be running the business now and I want to learn about it."

"What about school?" Man, I sounded like an old person.

"Don't worry, I'm coming back. I want to go to Boston College and major in business. They have a program for Corporate Social Responsibility. It's really cool. I can still do voice and theater too, but no more Michael. I'm over him."

"Really?" I asked.

"Well, I will be anyway. I mean, I definitely don't want to be in a relationship with someone who lies to get what he wants. Who knows what other bad stuff he would do!"

At dinner Hank toasted me and Toryn (in absentia; he was out with Eric) for our bravery. I knew he thought we were clumsy and foolhardy, but his smile was broad, like maybe he acknowledged my help just a little.

I asked about the investigation. Hank said they didn't have a confession, but it looked like Niles had brought coffee and pastries on a visit to Anita the day after he arrived in Boston. Somehow he removed the EpiPens from the closest spots.

"He would have known where they were," Dani interjected. "He's helped cook at our house before and stuff."

Hank continued. "The cheese Danish was hiding powdered walnuts which he must have snuck under the cheese. It was enough to kill her almost instantly."

Dani was calm. She'd had time to process a lot of this, and was no doubt relieved to have the truth known.

"Were Dob and Daniel Howser connected to it?" I asked.

"Not to killing Anita, but Dob was using gems as currency in illegal art deals, and he wanted to be the US distribution outlet for the Nayaks' gem trade. Howser was just one of his corrupt business associates. The problem was that Anita owned a controlling share of the business and he owned nothing. He and Niles couldn't move their plans for US distribution forward with her disapproval."

"But we don't believe Dob was complicit in murder," Jenny clarified.

"What about Brian?" Dani asked. "Did Niles kill him?"

"That's still under investigation," Hank said, "but we believe he hired it out if he didn't do it himself."

"Why?"

"It turned out Niles had Anita's computer. He probably saw communications between Anita and Brian indicating that there had been a lot of friction over the business. We think the reason Brian was trying to find the computer was that he was onto something and wanted more evidence that Niles was unhappy with Anita's involvement since she inherited her share of the business. We think Niles realized that Brian was figuring it out."

After dinner we sipped eggnog by the Christmas tree. Jenny checked my injuries and I basked in her attention, proud of my war wounds.

I thought about love I'd fought for and love I hadn't. I decided I wouldn't make any decisions about Will just yet. I remembered Gloria's advice—*you have to be willing to bleed.*

I excused myself from the living room, stepping away from the popping fire and the smell of the Christmas tree, out onto the porch overlooking the cedar and pine woods behind the house. I suppressed a shiver, accepting the bracing air. The moon was a slim crescent and stars pricked a dark crystal sky.

I dialed Marco.

Coming soon: **Penny Legend,** *book two of the Penny Wade mystery series.*

CHAPTER ONE

Which is worse, to be named after a worthless coin or to be saddled with a name like Legend?

Legend was escorted to my office by a young Boston cop on a Tuesday afternoon. I'd been alerted that he had a bullet graze wound on his leg, but I barely detected a limp when he walked in. The school principal had told the police that Legend was eight years old and he wasn't talking today.

His first stop after his teacher discovered the wound had been the Mass General ER; second stop, me.

"Legend, my name is Penny Wade," I said. "You can call me Penny. I'm a social worker, which means I help people like you when they have difficult stuff happen."

The cop, a petite, copper-haired woman around my age—mid-thirties—kneeled to say goodbye. Legend didn't make eye contact with her. She gave me a smile and left.

"Come sit?" I said.

When I'd gotten the call that he was coming, I'd culled the fidget toys on my table and added more play therapy toys. I had snow globes, rubber and wire animals for twisting, a cluster of magnet balls, tiny worry dolls, a couple of squishy stress balls, a mini Slinky, some toy cars, and a few natural things with nice textures—sea shells, stones, and driftwood.

Legend eyed the toys as he sidestepped slowly to my worn couch. His shoulders were drawn up practically to his ears.

"They're for you to play with."

No answer. He sat on the edge of the sofa, eyes cast down showing long curly dark eyelashes. I sat on the chair across from him.

Before I could say anything more, there was a knock at my office door. I rose to answer and found another police officer—a skinny Latin-looking guy with his thumbs in his belt.

"Hang on," I said to the officer.

I went to my desk and grabbed a stack of coloring sheets and a big box of crayons. I cleared a spot on the table and set them down for Legend.

"I'll be back in a minute. If you like to color you can choose something to color, okay?"

Legend nodded and I considered it my first victory.

In the hallway, the cop and I stepped away from my door.

"Officers paid a visit to Legend's guardian—his aunt—to try to find out how he was wounded. They found her in possession of drugs. She's been taken into custody." He was shifting his weight from side to side as he spoke. I thought he'd rather be elsewhere.

"Where's his mom?"

"Dead."

"Where's his dad?"

"Unknown. Aunt says the kid's never known him."

"Is there other family? Grandma? Anyone?"

"All we can determine is an uncle—the brother to mom and aunt—but he's only twenty and probably not a custodial candidate."

"Where's the Department of Children and Families in this?"

"We've contacted them and they're looking for an emergency foster placement."

I thanked the officer and paused for a minute in the hallway. If I didn't tell Legend what had happened I wasn't sure who would, or how well they'd handle the task.

When I stepped back into my office Legend was sitting on the floor by the coffee table coloring. I sat on the floor across from him and watched. He had chosen a picture of a mom and baby zebra. He colored only the grass and flowers around the zebras, then set down his crayon and pushed the paper toward me with a nod.

He had a point.

I picked up the picture. "Nice job. What do you think the zebras are going to do today?"

Legend's eyes flicked to mine for just an instant.

He didn't answer.

"You might be wondering about the police officer at my door," I said. "He came to tell me that when the police went to talk to your aunt about your wound, well, they realized they needed to talk with her some more—they need her help— so they asked her to go to the police station. They're trying to make sure everyone is safe after the shooting last night."

I was watching him closely but there wasn't much to see. He was listening but not reacting.

"After we talk you get to go back to school and these really nice people at a place called the Department of Children and Families are going to find a good place for you to stay tonight—kind of like a sleepover."

He kept his eyes down. He was remarkably still, holding a throw pillow in front of him.

"So here's the thing," I said. "I'm going to be your friend and help you with whatever you need."

His eyes met mine. I could see his pain and also something brave. He looked down again and set the pillow aside.

When the female officer returned to take Legend back to school I'd gotten one nod and a few seconds of eye contact. It wasn't exactly the information on who held the gun that Boston PD would be hoping for, but they were going to have to wait or figure it out some other way. There was a lot going on under those curly eyelashes and Legend was going to need time.

That afternoon a boy-next-door-handsome detective came to my office. Tall, sandy, bluish eyes, superhero-square jaw. He was wearing faded jeans that didn't hide the muscular lines of his thighs, and a dark T-shirt.

"Ms. Wade, I'm Detective Connor. I'm here about Legend Harris."

I showed him into my office, where he sat in the straight chair, casting a suspicious eye at my table full of toys.

"An officer was here earlier and told me Legend's aunt has been taken into custody. He explained that Mom is dead, Dad is unknown, and there's only a young uncle somewhere. That's all I know. I'll help however I can."

Detective Connor set one ankle onto the other knee. When he met my eyes he held them. "There was a murder on the street outside their apartment last night. A drug dealer. Naturally when we learned of the boy's wound we wondered if there was a connection. The victim was his aunt's boyfriend. Name of James Booker."

"What did his aunt say?"

"Desiree Platt. Not much. We had a warrant ready given the likelihood of a connection. We found twenty-five grams of OxyContin and some other pharmaceuticals. She claims she had nothing to do with it, but it's her apartment."

"But what did she say about Legend?"

"She said they were on the street with Mr. Booker and ran inside as fast as possible when the violence broke out. Legend was nicked by a stray bullet. She claims not to have seen the perp."

"Do you know what happened to Legend's mom?"

"Trinity Harris. Overdose. Two years ago."

I picked up a little doll from my table and fixed her hair while I let that sink in. "They took him back to school, right? Has DCF found a foster home?"

"He's at the school office until we find a placement." He uncrossed his legs and leaned toward me.

"Ms. Wade, we're going to need your cooperation on this investigation. Mr. Booker wasn't big-time, but we want to find his connections and the method of diversion."

"Diversion?"

"How pharmaceuticals go from legal to illegal channels of distribution."

"What can I do?"

"There's a good chance the boy saw who shot Mr. Booker. We want to know."

"But this is a narcotics investigation, not murder? You're a narcotics detective?"

"I'm in the Narcotics division, but that doesn't preclude me from investigating the entirety of the case. There's a homicide detective assigned to the case as well, Detective Polk."

"If you weren't worried about the drug crime would there even be a murder investigation?"

"Of course there would," he said. "I can't tell you how Homicide is handling their end of the investigation. Drugs are involved, so the Narcotics division is front and center."

I wondered if Homicide was doing anything at all.

"My priority is Legend," I said. "He isn't talking right now, at all. I may not be able to help you."

He rose and extended his hand. "I trust that you'll try."

Gloria, my roomie, was sprawled out on the couch in a tank top and underwear when I got home. Her big hair was bigger and kinkier than ever, spread over the arm of the couch above her head. Ranger, our one-eyed almost-black cat, was curled up at the other end of the couch—the dot at the bottom of Gloria's exclamation mark. The windows were open. It was only June and we couldn't afford to start running the A/C already despite the heat wave. It felt like the heat was bouncing right off the building three feet from ours and in through the open window.

My walk from the office didn't clear my frustration and I hoped a beer would help. I grabbed two from the fridge, opened them, and handed one to Gloria.

"How was work?" I asked. I'd been trying to do a better job remembering to ask about her day instead of dumping mine on her. Managing a chi-chi spa in the Back Bay had its own set of intrigues.

"Pretty typical. There was a big hen party of regulars so the staff is beat, but nothing went too wrong."

"Did something go a little wrong?"

"Mrs. Hampton's hair turned out a bit, well, coral, but we kept the lighting dim for relaxation so she hadn't noticed yet when she left. What happened with you? Why the beer?"

I'd stripped down to my T-shirt and capris and was considering going down to underwear like Gloria. "Is anyone coming over?"

"Yeah, Justin will later. He won't care if you're in underwear if that's what you're thinking."

"I thought I drove men wild."

"Mostly when I'm not in the room." She smiled.

I swigged my beer, took a deep breath, and told Gloria about Legend.

"Anyway, I'll sort out a therapy plan for him tomorrow, but I have narcs crawling down my back trying to get me to drag it out of him who shot him." I took another drink and noticed the beer was half gone. "Sorry to lay it on you. I'm just frustrated."

"You're a good therapist for him. I'm sure you'll help. Besides, I read that like ninety-five percent of communication is nonverbal."

"Hey, can I borrow your mini trampoline for my office for a little while? Kid that size has a lot of jumpiness, you know? Maybe it will help him to bounce."

"Yep, and we'll make that purple dyed rice and scent it with lavender for him to play with too. Cute kid?"

"Real cute."

Justin buzzed up from downstairs and I headed to my room to make some notes on the ideas I had for working with Legend. I'd taken some play therapy classes in college and was excited to put them to use. Legend had a traumatic experience. I could deal with that. I just needed to block out the noise and focus on the kid.

Will, my long-time on/off boyfriend, called as I was getting ready for bed that night. I told him about my day. He didn't want to talk about his work—he was a frustrated artist working in graphic design—but we talked about his garden and the great sailing weather in Madison.

"I'd like to come out if you want me to. I have some time off banked," he said.

I'd seen him a few weeks before when I went to Madison for Memorial Day weekend. We were doing well together, but that made me kind of nervous because I'm not the greatest with relationships. "Great!" It sounded a little forced. I hope he didn't notice because I really was happy he was coming. "When?"

We hatched a plan for him to come to Boston and said goodnight. I lay in bed worrying about whether I could be the girlfriend he wanted. I pictured us in his storybook house on the outskirts of Madison. I imagined us in the kitchen with harvest from the huge garden. Sounds of the children laughing and playing in the yard would drift in the open window. We would can tomatoes and pickle okra and green beans. We'd talk and laugh while we shelled peas and shucked corn with our yellow Lab curled at our feet snoozing. It would be a good life, solid and healthy for kids. Surely I could learn to pickle, and tolerate a rural home, and like dogs.

I'd have to figure that out later. First I needed to focus on Legend. Something told me this could get complicated and he was going to need someone firmly on his side.

ABOUT THE AUTHOR

Lucy English is an author, sociologist, and dreamer. She lives in St. Louis, Missouri with her two sons.

To learn more visit
www.pennywademysteries.com